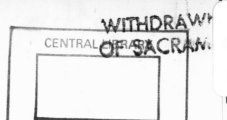

A Few Last Words

A Few Last Words

James Sallis

THE MACMILLAN COMPANY

ACKNOWLEDGMENTS

Letter to a Young Poet, A Few Last Words, The History Makers, The Creation of Bennie Good, Jim and Mary G, Copyright © 1968, 1968, 1969, 1970, 1970 by Damon Knight. Originally appeared in *Orbit.*

Faces, Hands, Copyright © 1970 by Harry Harrison. Originally appeared in *Nova 1* (as *Faces & Hands*).

Slice of Universe, Copyright © 1968 by Ultimate Publishing Co., Inc.

Kazoo, Bubbles, Jeremiad, Front & Centaur, Copyright © 1967, 1968, 1969, 1970 by *New Worlds.*

The Anxiety in the Eyes of the Cricket, Copyright © 1969 by James Sallis. Originally appeared in *The New S.F.,* ed. Langdon Jones (Hutchinson & Co., Ltd.: London).

And then the dark—, Copyright © 1969 by James Sallis. Originally appeared in *The War Book* (Rupert Hart-Davis Ltd.: London).

The Opening of the Terran Ballet, Enclave, Occasions, Jane Crying, Copyright © 1970 by James Sallis.

In addition the author should like to thank the following:

Alfred A. Knopf, Inc., for permission to quote from *The Rock,* from *The Collected Poems of Wallace Stevens,* Copyright © 1954 by Wallace Stevens.

Grove Press, Inc., for permission to quote form Richard Howard's translation of *Last Year at Marienbad* (*L'Année Dernière à Marienbad*), text by Alain Robbe-Grillet for the film by Alain Resnais, Copyright © 1962 by Grove Press, Inc.

Clayton Eshleman and *TriQuarterly* for permission to quote the lines of Vincente Huidobro, first English-language appearance in *TriQuarterly 15,* Copyright © 1969 by Northwestern University Press.

Copyright © 1970 by James Sallis

The Macmillan Company
866 Third Avenue, New York, N. Y. 10022
Collier-Macmillan Canada Ltd., Toronto, Ontario

Library of Congress Catalog Card Number: 71–122293

First Printing

Printed in the United States of America

FOR KATE AND DAMON
AND FOR PAM

—dans les ans nous trouvons quelque content

CONTENTS

AVANT-PROPOS

It makes so little difference. . . .
. . . where one looks, one has been there before.

Wallace Stevens

The lives they lived in the mind are at an end.
They never were.

Wallace Stevens

Don't give them any name. . . . They could have had so
many other adventures.

Alain Robbe-Grillet

Invent new worlds
& be careful what you say.

Vincente Huidobro

JIM AND MARY G

Getting his little coat down off the hook, then his arms into it, not easy because he's so excited and he always turns the wrong way anyhow. And all the time he's looking up at you with those blue eyes. We go park Papa, he says. We go see gulls. Straining for the door. The gulls are a favorite; he discovered them on the boat coming across and can't understand, he keeps looking for them in the park.

Wrap the muffler around his neck. Yellow, white. (Notice how white the skin is there, how the veins show through.) They call them scarves here don't they. Stockingcap—he pulls it down over his eyes, going Haha. He hasn't learned to laugh yet. Red mittens. Now move the zipper up and he's packed away. The coat's green corduroy, with black elastic at the neck and cuffs and a round hood that goes down over the cap. It's November. In England. Thinking, The last time I'll do this. Is there still snow on the ground, I didn't look this morning.

Take his hand and go on out of the flat. Letting go at the door because it takes two hands to work the latch, Mary rattling dishes in the kitchen. (Good-bye, she says very softly as you shut the door.) He goes around you and beats you to the front door, waits there with his nose on the glass. The hall is full of white light. Go on down it to him. The milk's come, two bottles, with the *Guardian* leaning between them. Move the mat so we can open the door, We go park Papa, we seegulls. Frosty foggy air coming in. Back for galoshes, all the little brass-tongue buckles? No the snow's gone. Just some dirty slush. Careful. Down the steps.

Crunching down the sidewalk ahead of you, disappointed because there's no snow but looking back, Haha. We go park? The sky is flat and white as a sheet of paper. Way off, a flock of birds goes whirling across it, circling inside themselves—black dots, like iron filings with a magnet under the paper. The block opposite is lined with trees. What kind? The leaves are all rippling together. It looks like green foil. Down the walk.

Asking, Why is everything so still. Why aren't there any cars. Or a mailtruck. Or milkcart, gliding along with bottles jangling. Where is everyone. It's ten in the morning, where is everyone.

But there is a car just around the corner, stuck on ice at the side of the road where it parked last night with the wheels spinning Whrrrrr. Smile, you understand a man's problems. And walk the other way. His mitten keeps coming off in your hand. Haha.

She had broken down only once, at breakfast.

The same as every morning, the child had waked them. Standing in his bed in the next room and bouncing up and down till the springs were banging against the frame. Then he climbed out and came to their door, peeking around the frame, finally doing his tiptoe shyly across the floor in his white wool nightshirt. Up to their bed, where they pretended to be still asleep. Brekpust, Brekpust, he would say, poking at them and tugging the covers, at last climbing onto the bed to bounce up and down between them until they rolled over: Hello. Morninggg. He is proud of his g's. Then, Mary almost broke down, remembering what today was, what they had decided the night before.

She turned her face toward the window (they hadn't been able to afford curtains yet) and he heard her breathe deeply several times. But a moment later she was up—out of bed in her quilted robe and heading for the kitchen, with the child behind her.

He reached and got a cigarette off the trunk they were using as a night table. It had a small wood lamp, a bra, some single cigarettes and a jarlid full of ashes and filters on it. Smoking, listening to water running, pans clatter, cupboards and drawers. Then the sounds stopped and he heard them together in the bathroom: the tap ran for a while, then the toilet flushed and he heard the child's pleased exclamations. They went back into the kitchen and the sounds resumed. Grease crackling, the child chattering about how good he had been. The fridge door opened and shut, opened again, Mary said something. He was trying to help.

He got out of bed and began dressing. How strange that she'd forgotten to take him to the bathroom first thing, she'd never done that before. Helpinggg, from the kitchen by way of explanation, as he walked to the bureau. It was square and ugly, with that shininess peculiar to cheap furniture, and it had been in the flat when they moved in, the only thing left behind. He opened a drawer and took out a shirt. All his shirts were white. Why, she had once asked him, years ago. He didn't know, then or now.

He went into the kitchen with the sweater over his head. "Mail?" Through the wool. Neither of them looked around, so he pulled it the rest of the way on, reaching down inside to tug the shirtcollar out. Then the sleeves.

"A letter from my parents. They're worried they haven't heard from us, they hope we're all right. Daddy's feeling better, why don't we write them."

The child was dragging his highchair across the floor from the corner. Long ago they had decided he should take care of as many of his own needs as he could—a sense of responsibility, Mary had said—but this morning Jim helped him carry the chair to the table, slid the tray off, lifted him into it and pushed the chair up to the table. When he looked up, Mary turned quickly away, back to the stove.

Eggs, herring, toast and ham. "I thought it would be nice," Mary said. "To have a good breakfast." And that was the time she broke down.

The child had started scooping the food up in his fingers, so she got up again and went across the kitchen to get his spoon. It was heavy silver, with an ivory *K* set into the handle, and it had been her own. She turned and came back across the tile, holding the little spoon in front of her and staring at it. Moma cryinggg, the child said. Moma cryinggg. She ran out of the room. The child turned in his chair to watch her go, then turned back and went on eating with the spoon. The plastic padding squeaked as the child moved inside it. The chair was metal, the padding white with large blue asterisks all over it. They had bought it at a Woolworths. Twelve and six. Like the bureau, it somehow fit the flat.

A few minutes later Mary came back, poured coffee for both of them and sat down across from him.

"It's best this way," she said. "He won't have to suffer. It's the only answer."

He nodded, staring into the coffee. Then took off his glasses and cleaned them on his shirttail. The child was stirring the eggs and herring together in his bowl. Holding the spoon like a chisel in his hand and going round and round the edge of the bowl.

"Jim. . . ."

He looked up. She seemed to him, then, very tired, very weak.

"We could take him to one of those places. Where they . . . take care of them . . . for you."

He shook his head, violently. "No, we've already discussed that, Mary. He wouldn't understand. It will be easier, my way. If I do it myself."

She went to the window and stood there watching it. It filled most of one wall. It was frosted over.

"How would you like to go for a walk after breakfast," he asked the child. He immediately shoved the bowl away and said, "Bafroom first?"

"You or me?" Mary said from the window.

Finally: "You."

He sat alone in the kitchen, thinking. Taps ran, the toilet flushed, he came out full of pride. "We go park," he said. "We go see gulls."

"Maybe." It was this, the lie, which came back to him later; this was what he remembered most vividly. He got up and walked into the hall with the child following him and put his coat on. "Where's his other muffler?"

"In the bureau drawer. The top one."

He got it, then began looking for the stockingcap and mittens. Walking through the rooms, opening drawers. There aren't any seagulls in London. When she brought the cap and mittens to him there was a hole in the top of the cap and he went off looking for the other one. Walking through rooms, again and again into the child's own.

"For God's sake go on," she finally said. "Please stop. O damn Jim, go on." And she turned and ran back into the kitchen.

Soon he heard her moving about. Clearing the table, running water, opening and shutting things. Silverware clicking.

"We go park?"

He began to dress the child. Getting his little coat down off the hook. Wrapping his neck in the muffler. There aren't any seagulls in London. Stockingcap, Haha.

Thinking, This is the last time I'll ever do this.

Now bump, bump, bump. Down the funny stairs.

When he returned, Mary was lying on the bed, still in the quilted robe, watching the ceiling. It seemed very dark, very cold in the room. He sat down beside her in his coat and put his hand on her arm. Cars moved past the window. The people upstairs had their radio on.

"Why did you move the bureau?" he asked after a while.

Without moving her head she looked down toward the foot of the bed. "After you left I was lying here and I noticed a traffic light or something like that out on the street was reflected in it. It was blinking on and off, I must have watched it for an hour. We've been here for weeks and I never saw that before. But once I did, I had to move it."

"You shouldn't be doing heavy work like that."

For a long while she was still, and when she finally moved, it was just to turn her head and look silently into his face.

He nodded, once, very slowly.

"It didn't. . . ."

No.

She smiled, sadly, and still in his coat, he lay down beside her in the small bed. She seemed younger now, rested, herself again. There was warmth in her hand when she took his own and put them together on her stomach.

They lay quietly through the afternoon. Ice was reforming on the streets; outside, they could hear wheels spinning, engines racing. The hall door opened, there was a jangle of milkbottles, the door closed. Then everything was quiet. The trees across the street drooped under the weight of the ice.

There was a sound in the flat. Very low and steady, like a ticking. He listened for hours before he realized it was the drip of a faucet in the bathroom.

Outside, slowly, obscuring the trees, the night came. And with it, snow. They lay together in the darkness, looking out the frosted window. Occasionally, lights moved across it.

"We'll get rid of his things tomorrow," she said after a while.

I

Letter to a Young Poet

Dear James Henry,

   This morning your letter, posted from Earth over two
years ago, at last reached me, having from all indications
passed through the most devious of odysseys: at one
point, someone had put the original envelope (battered
and confused with stampings and re-addressings) into
another, addressed it by hand, and paid the additional
postage. You wonder what word suits the clerk who sal-
vaged your letter from the computer dumps and took it
upon himself to do this. Efficiency? Devotion? Largesse?
Gentilesse?

   At any rate, by the time it finally reached me here, the

new envelope was as badly in need of repair as your own. I can't imagine the delay; I shouldn't think I'd be so hard a man to find. I move around a lot, true, but always within certain well-defined borders. Like Earth birds that never stray past a mile from their birth tree, I live my life in parentheses. . . . I suppose it's just that no one especially bothers to keep track.

For your kind words I can only say: thank you. Which is not enough, never enough, but what else is there? (Sometimes, as with our mysterious and gracious postal patron, even that is impossible.) It makes me happy to learn that my poems have brought you pleasure. If they've given you something else as well, which you say they have, I am yet happier. You have expressed your joy at my sculpture. That also makes me happy. Thank you.

In brief answer to your questions, I am now living in Juhlz on Topfthar, the northernmost part of the Vegan Combine, though I don't know how much longer I shall be here. Political bickering breeds annoying restrictions and begins to throw off a deafening racket—and after four years the Juhlzson winter is at last creeping in (I'm sitting out on my patio now; I can see it far off in the hills). The two together, I'm afraid I can't withstand.

The hours of my day hardly vary. I rise to a breakfast of bread and wine, pass the day fiddling at my books. I rarely write, sculpt even less, the preparation is so difficult. . . . Night is a time for music and talking in Juhlz cafés, which are like no others. (The casual asymmetry of Juhlzson architecture always confounds the Terran eye. The people are like the buildings, off-center, beautiful. You never know what to expect.) I have taken up a local instrument—the thulinda, a kind of aeolian harp or perhaps dulcimer, fitted to a mouthpiece—and have got, I am told, passably good. I play for them and they teach me their songs.

(The sky's just grown gray cumulus beards and a voice like a bass siren. It should snow, but won't. My paper flaps and flutters against the table. Darkness begins to seep around the edges. This is dusk on Juhlz, my favorite time of day.)

As to your other questions, I was born on Earth: my first memories are of black, occluded skies and unbearable temperatures, and my parents fitting filters to my face when, rarely, we went outside (my poem, Eve Mourning).

My father was a microbiologist. Soon after I was born, he became a Voyager; I remember him hardly at all, and his hands mostly, at that. My mother, as you probably know since one of my publishers made a thing of it quite against my wishes, was Vegan, a ship's companion, a woman whose gentle voice and quiet hands could do more than any medic to soothe a hurt, salve a scar. They met during a Voyage my father took in place of a friend —his first—and were together always after that. One of my early sculptures, Flange Coupling, was realized as a memorial to my parents. I don't know if you've seen it. The last I heard, it was in a private collection on Rigel-7. But that was years and years ago.

My early life was spent in comfort, in my grandparents' home on Vega and other times in crèches on Earth. When I was seven, my parents were killed in Exploration; shortly after, I was sent to the Academy at Ginh, where I passed my next twelve years and for which the Union provided funds and counsel. My *Letters Home,* which

I've come in past years to misdoubt, was an attempt to commemorate that time, at least to invest it with private worth.

I don't know what command you have of Vegan history; I suppose when I was a young man I cared nothing for history of any sort. But these were the years of the Quasitots, who supposed themselves a political group and spent their time and talents in metaphorical remonstrance against the mercenary trends of Vegan–Outworld affairs. (If I am telling you things you already know, please forgive me, but what looms large on my horizon may be unseen from yours; I have no way of knowing.)

In one of the "Letters" I quoted Naevius, an early Roman poet (my interest in Latin being perhaps the sole solid tie I have with my father's world). . . . "Q. Tell me, how was your great commonwealth lost so quickly? A. We were overrun by a new lot of orators, a bunch of silly youngsters." I believe we thought that fitted us. We answered their declarations and old speeches with avant-garde aesthetics; we thought we would be the "silly youngsters" who'd usher in a new order. I suppose, vaguely, we believed that artists should inherit the universe.

One of my friends at the Academy took to composing symphonies of odor, the foulest odors he could find and produce, dedicating each work to the two governments. Another created an artificial flower which would wilt if touched; yet another gathered dung and baked it into likenesses of the Heads of State. My own contribution (half-hearted at best, I suppose) was the sculpting of single grains of sand, using the tools of my father, then scattering my invisible beauty in handfuls wherever I walked.

I'm not certain any longer what we really thought we were accomplishing. In our own words we were reacting, we were speaking out, we were being ourselves, we were caring. At any rate, this activity channeled our energies, made us work, made us think, let us live off of each other's various frenzies. It taught some of us, a few, that words and gestures get nothing done. Maybe somewhere, somehow, it accomplished something larger; I don't know. (I understand, by the way, that microsculpture is quite the thing in the academies today.) Such, anyway, was the temper and tempo of my youth.

When I was twenty, I left Ginh with my degrees and came to live in a small room up four flights of stairs here on Juhlz (my poem, *Crown of Juhlz*). I worked for a while as a tutor, then held a position at the old Empire Library, but came very soon to realize that I was unable to fit myself to a job of any sort.

I fled to Farthay, where I wrote my first novel and married. She was a young, small thing with joy in her heart and light in her eyes, a Vegan. Two years with me, and without the comfort of a child, was all she could bear. She left. It was best for both of us. We had already spent too much of our separate selves.

The rest of my life (I am 84) has been spent in forming and breaking idle patterns. I travel a lot, settle for short periods, move on (your letter retraced, and made me remember, many years of my life). What money I have comes through the kindness of friends; and from other, distant friends who buy my books.

My books: you ask after them. Thank you. Well, there's *Letters Home*, which I've already mentioned and which you've probably read. Quite against my own preferences and wishes, it has proved my most popular book; I've been told that it's taught in literature and sociology classes round about the Union.

There are the novels: *Day Breaks; Pergamum* (a sort of eulogy for my marriage); *A Throw of the Dice; Fugue and Imposition;* one or two others I'd just as soon not admit to.

Essays: *Pillow Saint; Halfway Houses; Arcadias; Avatars and Auguries.* Two volumes of letters between the Vegan poet Arndto and myself, concerning mostly Outworld poetry, entitled *Rosebushes* and *Illuminations.*

A collection of short stories, three volumes, *Instants of Desertion.*

And of course, the poems . . . *Overtures and Paradiddles; Misericords; Poems; Negatives; Abyssinia; Poems* again; *Printed Circuits; Assassins of Polish.* Some while back, I received a check with a letter informing me that a *Collected Poems* was to be issued through Union Press. I can't recall just how long ago that was, and can't know how long the message took to find me, so I don't know whether the book is available.

And coming at last to the poems you've sent, what am I to say? All critical intent is beyond me, I fear. I've been constantly bemused and confounded by what critics have found to praise and damn in my own work: I was aware neither that I had "narrowly ordered my sensibilities" nor that I "struck out boldly into the perilous waters that lie between a poetry of device and the poetry of apocalypse" (which another renders as aiming between "a poem of sentiment and one of structure"). Give me always the Common Reader, the sensitive ignorance.

("The perilous waters" . . . had I known there was danger of drowning, I might never have begun to write.)

You want Authority; I can give you none. Let me in-

stead look up at these winter-blurred hills and say this:
the poems you've sent, and which I return with this letter
—they are not unique, but they speak of something which
may come, something which may become yours alone.
Perhaps you have it now. But two years is a very short
time.

They are direct, compact, all the flourishes are beneath
the surface—things greatly to be praised in a young
writer. In one line you are content to give shape, in
another you pause and form; always something comes
easy, to the ear, the eye, the tongue, the mind, the heart.
Also to be admired.

You evidently achieve control with little struggle, effective structure with somewhat more difficulty (precision
and accuracy are often separate things). But you have
patience, and this will come. Your diction draws crisp,
sharp lines around a poem, while imagery and resonance
make what is contained soft and yielding. This is at least a
proper direction. And I think you are right to work from
the outside in, the way you seem to do.

Two years ago, when you wrote the letter, you were
looking for an older, wiser, gentler voice than your own. I
am sorry that I have been so long in admitting that I
cannot provide it. Perhaps you've already found one, in
some academy, some café. Or perhaps you no longer need
it; edges have a way of wearing off. Peace, calm—but
what I can give you is closer to a stillness.

I was quite moved by the Betelgeuse mood poems in
particular: I should say that. I envy you these poems.
Because of a late-developing nervous disorder, a clash in
my mixed parentage, I am confined pretty much to Vega.
I've not been outside the Combine since the day I came
here. Something in the specific light complements my

affliction, and I can go on in good health. But I believe I shall have to return to dark Earth before I die, that at least, in spite of all.

It occurs to me that you obviously know about writing, and I think you must have known the worth of your poems, so I can only assume that you are really asking about living. And I have one thing to say, a quiet thing: Ally yourself to causes and people, and you'll leave bits of yourself behind every step you take; keep it all, and you'll choke on it. The choice is every man's, for himself.

The day is wearing down, burning near its end. Lights have gone on then off again in the houses around me. Everyone is feeling alone.

So as darkness and winter move in, hand in hand, let me wish you the best of luck in your ambitions, apologize again for the delay, and bring to a close this letter, longer than any letter has a right to be.

And in closing, please accept again my thanks for your kind words. They are given so easily, yet mean so much, always.

Night now. Juhlzson birds have come off the lakes and out of forests, and are throbbing softly around me. The moons are sailing in and out of clouds. In a moment I shall move off the patio into the house. In a moment.

Yours,
Samthar Smith

Faces, Hands

KETTLE OF STARS

A lot of Couriers are from academic backgrounds, everything from literature to energy mechanics, the idea being that intellectual hardening of the arteries is less likely to occur if you watch what you eat and keep the blood flowing. You have to stay flexible: one loose word, one unguarded reaction, and you've not only lost respect and a job, you've probably thrown an entire world out of sympathy with Earth. In those days a Courier was a kind of bargainlot diplomat/prime minister/officeboy, and we were playing most of it by ear; we hadn't been in Union long enough to set standards. So when they started the Service they took us out of the classrooms, out of the lines that stood waiting for diplomas—because we were sup-

posed to know things like unity being the other side of a
coin called variety. Knowledge, they assumed, breeds tol-
erance. Or at least caution.

Dr. Desai (Comparative Cultural) used to lean out
over the podium he carried between classrooms to pro-
claim: "All the institutions, the actions, the outrages and
distinctions of an era find their equivalent in any other
era." He said it with all the conviction of a politician
making the rounds before General Conscript, his small
face bobbing up and down to emphasize every word. I
took my degree at Arktech under Desai, and in my three
years there I must have heard him say that a hundred
times: everything else he—or any other instructor—said,
built back up to it like so many stairsteps. A zikkurat:
climb any side, you get to the top. Some early member of
the Service must have had Dr. Desai too. They had the
same thing in mind.

For me it was June, on a day like yellow crystal. I was
sitting in an outdoor café across from the campus with my
degree rolled up in a pocket, cup half full of punjil, myself
brimful of insouciance. It was a quiet day, with the wind
pushing about several low blue clouds. I was looking
across at the towers and grass of the Academy, thinking
about ambition—what was it like to have it? I had no
desire to teach: I couldn't get past Desai's sentence. And
for similar reasons I was reluctant to continue my studies.
An object at rest stays at rest, and I was very much at rest.

Distractedly, I had been watching a small man in
Vegan clothes work his way down along the street, stopping to peer into each shop in turn. When finally he
reached the café, he looked around, saw me in the corner
and began smiling. I barely had time to stand before he

was at the table, hand stuck out, briefcase already opening.

Like Desai, he was a little man, forehead and chin jutting back from a protruding nose.

"Hello, Lant," he said. "I was told I could probably find you over here." He sat down across from me. He had small red eyes, like a rabbit's. "Let me introduce myself: Golfanth Stein. S-t-e-i-n: stain. I wonder if you've heard the Council's organizing a new branch." I hadn't. "Now that we're in Union there's a certain problem in representation, you know. Much to be done, embassies to establish, ambassador work. So we're beginning the Courier Service. Your degree in anthropology, for instance. . . ."

He bought me a drink and I signed his papers.

Ten years . . . Ten years out of school, ten years spent climbing the webwork of diplomatic service—and I found it all coming back to me there on Alsfort, as I sat in the wayroom of the Court.

There was a strike in effect; some of you will remember it. A forced-landing had come down too hard, too fast, and the Wagon had snapped the padbrace like a twig, toppling a half-acre of leadsub over onto the firesquads. So the Court workers were striking for subsurface landings, for Pits. My inbound had been the last. They were being turned away to Flaghold now, the next-door (half a million miles away) neighbor, an emergency port.

And if you sat in a Court and sweated at what was going on a Jump-week behind you on Earth and two ahead of you, on Altar; if you cursed and tried to bribe the crews; if you sent endless notes to both ends of the line you were knotted on; or if perhaps you are a history student specializing in the Wars . . . you'll remember the strike. Otherwise, probably not. Alsfort isn't exactly a backyard—more like an oasis.

Two days, and I'd given up insisting, inquiring, begging. I'd even given up the notes.

So I sat in the wayroom drinking the local (and distant) relative of beer. The pouch was locked into my coat pocket and I was keeping my left arm against it. I spent the first day there worrying what might happen on Altar without that pouch, then I gave it up the way I'd given up trying to surmount the strike, to curtail my immobility and its likely disastrous consequences. I just sat and drank "beer" and punjil and watched the people.

There was a short, wiry man of Jewish blood, Earth or Vegan, who limped from a twisted back, as though all his life he'd been watching over his shoulder. He drank tea saturated with grape sugar at ten and four and took his meals as the clock instructed: noon, six. He wore skirts, and a corduroy skullcap he never removed.

There was a couple, definitely Vegan. The woman was old (though only in profile), dressed in Outworld furs and wearing a single jewel against her emphatic and no doubt plastic bosom—a different jewel each time I saw them. Her companion was young, beautiful and asthenic, always precisely dressed in a fine tight suit, and quite often scribbling in a notebook he carried. They came irregularly and drank Earth brandy. By the third day too much sameness had taken its toll: she sat with her face screwed into jealousy as he smiled and wrote in his book. When she spoke, there were quiet, gulping rhythms in her voice, and her only answer was the boy's beautiful smile and, once, a hand that held hers tightly—too tightly—on the table. He waited in the halls while she paid; she kept her face down, an older face now; they went away.

A Glaucon, a man I knew from Leic, but his ruby robes
signaled pilgrimage and forbade us to speak. I watched
him at his evening coffees. A recent convert, he was not at
all the craftsmanlike politician I had come to know in
those months spent on his world, in his home. He had
been quick, loud; now he plodded, and his voice followed
softly in the distance, muttering at prayer.

And there were others, many others. . . .

A Plethgan couple with a Vorsh baby, evidently returning home from the Agencies at Llarth. They came to the
wayroom just once, to ask about Vorshgan for the child,
and were told there was none. The mother was already
pale with fear, the father raging and helpless; the baby
screamed and was turning blue. They went out talking
quietly to themselves under the child's cries. I never saw
them again.

A Llyrch woman, alone and wearing only a formal
shawl. It was brown, showing midcaste. A single green
stripe and a small silver star proclaimed that her husband
was dead; that he died in honor, in a duel on Highker,
away from home. Once she turned in her seat and the
shawl fell partly open, exposing, beneath her hairless
head, exorcised breasts and the carvings in her belly. She
took nothing but water, and little of that.

And there was a man who came to the wayroom as
often as I and sat as long, sipping a pale violet liquid from
a crystal cup, reading or simply sitting, hands together,
staring at the wall and moving his lips softly. He was
short, with a quick smile and white teeth, hair gathered
with ribbons to one side of his head. I wondered what he
was drinking. He carried it in a flask to match the cup;
you could smell it across the room, a light scent, pale as its
color, subtle as perfume. Outworld, probably: he flat-

tened his vowels, was precisely polite; there were remnants of a drawl. Urban, from the way he carried himself, the polished edge of gestures. His mien and clothes were adopted from the Vegans, but that was common enough to be useless in reading origin, and might have been assumed solely for this trip. Vegan influence was virtually ubiquitous then, before the Wars. I generally travelled in Vegan clothes myself, even used the language. Most of us did. It was the best way to move about without being noticed.

The Outworlds, though. I was fairly sure of that. . . .

Lying out along the fringe of trade routes, they were in a unique position to Union civilization. Quite early they had developed a more or less static society, little touched by new influences spreading outward from Vega: by the time ripples had run that far, they were pretty weak. There was little communication other than political, little enough culture exchange that it didn't matter. The Outworld societies had gone so far and stopped; then, as static cultures will, become abstracted, involuted—picking out parts and making them wholes. Decadence, they used to call it.

Then the Vegans came up with the Drive, the second one, Overspace. And suddenly the Outworlds were no longer so Out, though they kept the name. The rest of us weren't long in discovering the furth's fur, shelby and punjil, which for a while threatened to usurp the ancient hierarchy of coffee and alcohol on Earth with its double function as both stimulant *and* depressant. Under this new deluge of ships and hands (giving, taking) the Outworlds were at last touched. They were, in fact, virtually struck in the face. And the Outworlds, suddenly, were in transition.

But there's always an Orpheus, always those who look back. Under the swing of transition now, decadence had come to full flower. Amid the passing of old artifice, old extravagance, dandyism had sprung up as a last burst of heroism, a protest against the changing moods.

And there was much about the man I watched—the way his plain clothes hung, something about his hair and the subtly padded chest, his inviolable personality and sexlessness; books held up off the table, away from his eyes—that smacked of dandyism. It's the sort of thing a Courier learns to look for.

There were others, fleeting and constant. Single; coupled; even one Medusa-like Gafrt symb in which I counted five distinct bodies, idly wondering how many others had been already assimilated. But these I've mentioned are the ones I still think about, recalling their faces, the hollow forms hands made in air, their voices filling those forms. The ones I felt, somehow, I knew. These—and one other. . . .

Rhea.

Without her Alsfort wouldn't be for me the vivid memory it is. It would be a jumbled, distorted horror of disappointment, failure, confusing faces. A time when I sat still and the world walked past me and bashed its head into the wall.

Rhea.

I saw her once, the last day. For a handful of minutes we touched lives across a table. I doubt she remembers. For her now, there will have been so *many* faces. I doubt she remembers.

It was mid-afternoon of my fourth day on Alsfort. The strike was beginning to run down; that morning, perhaps from boredom, the workers had volunteered a bit of light, routine work away from the Wagons, just to keep the Court from clogging up beyond all hope. I watched them unpack, adjust, and test a new booster. One of the men climbed into it and with a hop went sailing out across the pads, flailing his arms violently. Minutes later, he came walking back across the gray expanse, limping and grinning. He went up to the engineer and began talking quietly, shaking his head and gesturing toward one of the leg extensions. They vanished together, still talking, into the tool shop, hauling the booster between them.

I had gone from lunch at the Mart to coffee from the lobby servicors. Settling into a corner I watched the people wander about the arcade—colors, forms, faces blurred by distance; grouping and dissolving, aimless abstract patterns. Going back to my room had been a bad experience: too quiet, too inviting of thought.

The landscape of Alsfort. . . .

You can see it from the rim in the top levels—though *see* is inappropriate. *Study* would be better: an exercise in optical monotony. Brown and gray begin at the base of the Court and blend to various tones of baldness, blankness. Brown and gray, rocks and sand—it all merges into itself. Undefined. You walk out on the floating radial arms, trying to get closer, to make it resolve at least to lines. But it simply lies there. Brown, gray, amorphous.

So, after the briefest of battles, I wound up back in the wayroom. There was a booth just off-center, provided with console-adjustment seats and a trick mirror. Sitting there, you had the private tables in front of you, quick-service counters behind. You could watch the tables and, by tilting your head and squinting, dimly see what went on behind you, at the counters. Through the door you

could watch people wandering the corridors. I had spent
most of my four days in that booth, washing down surro-
gate-tablets with beer and punjil. Mostly Energine: sleep
was impossible, or at least the silent hours of lying to wait
for sleep. And somehow the thought of food depressed me
almost as much. I tried to eat, ordering huge meals and
leaving them untouched. By the fourth day my thoughts
were a bit scrambled and I was beginning, mildly, to
hallucinate.

The waiter was bringing me a drink when she came in.
I was watching the mirror, hardly aware of his presence.
Behind me, a man was talking to a companion who flick-
ered in and out of sight; I was trying to decide whether
this was the man's hallucination or my own. The waiter
put my drink down with one hand, not watching, and
knocked it against the curb. Startled, I felt the cold on my
hands. I turned my head and saw what he was looking
at. . . .

Rhea.

She was standing in the doorway with the white floor
behind her, blue light swelling in around her body. *Poised*
was the word that came to me: she might fly at the first
sudden motion.

She was . . . delicate. That was the second impression.
A thing made of thinnest glass; too fine, too small, too
perfect. Maybe five feet. Thin. You felt you could take her
in your palm: she was that fine, that light. That fragile.

Tiny cameo feathers covered her body—scarlet, blue,
sungold. And when light struck them they shimmered,
threw off others, eyefuls of color. They thinned down her
limbs and grew richer in tone; her face and hands were
bare, white. And above the small carved face were other

feathers: dark blue plumes, almost black, that brushed on her shoulders as she walked—swayed and danced.

Her head darted on air to survey the room. Seeing my eyes on her she smiled, then started through the tables. She moved like leaves in wind, hands fluttered at her sides, fingers long and narrow as blades of grass. Feathers swayed with her, against her, spilling chromatic fire.

And suddenly karma or the drugs or just my loneliness —whatever it was—had me by the shoulders and was tugging, pulling.

I came to myself, the room forming out of confusion, settling into a square fullness. I was standing there away from the booth, I was saying, "Could I buy you a drink?" My hand almost . . . almost at her shoulder. The bones there delicate as a bird's breast.

She stood looking back past me, then up at my face, into my eyes, and smiled again. Her own eyes were light orange beneath thin hard lids that blinked steadily, sliding over the eyes and back up, swirled with colors like the inside of seashells.

"Yes, thank you," in Vegan. "It would be very nice. Of you." She sang the words. Softly. I doubt that anyone but myself heard them.

I looked back at the Outworlder. He had been watching; now he frowned and returned to his book.

"I was tired. Of the room," she said, rustling into the booth. "I said. To him. I could not stay there, some time ago, much longer. I would like to come, here. And see the people."

"Him?"

"My . . . escort? Karl. That the room was. Not pretty, it made me sad. The bare walls, your walls are such . . .

solid. There is something sad about bare walls. Our own are hammered from bright metals, thin and, open. Covered with reliefs. The forms of, growing things. I should not have to. Stay, in the room?"

"No. You shouldn't." I moved my hand to activate the dampers. All sound outside the booth sank to a dull, low murmur like the sea far off, while motion continued, bringing as it always did a strange sense of isolation and unreality.

I ordered punjil. The waiter left and returned with a tall cone of bright green fluid, which he decanted off into two small round glasses. His lips moved but the dampers blocked the sound; getting no response, he went away.

"I'm Lant."

"Rhea," she said. "You are, Vegan?"

"Earth."

"You work. Here."

"No. Coming through, held up by the strike. You?"

She sipped the punjil. "It is, for me, the same. You are a, crewman? On one of the ships then."

"No. I'm with a travel bureau. Moving around as much as I can, keeping an eye out for new ports, new contracts." Later, somehow, I regretted the lies, that came so easily. "On my way Out. I think there might be some good connections out there."

"I've heard the cities are. Very beautiful."

"This is my first time Out in ten years." That part, at least, was true; I had gone Out on one of my first assignments. "They were beautiful, breathtaking, even then. And they've done a lot in the last few years, virtually rebuilt whole worlds. The largest eclecticism the Union's known—they've borrowed from practically every culture in *and* out of Union. . . . They're even building in crystals now. They say the cities look like glass blossoms, like flowers grown out of the ground. That there is nothing else like them."

"I saw a picture of Ginh, a painting, once. Like a man had made it in his hand and put it, into the trees. A lot of trees, all kinds. And sculpture, mosaics. In, the buildings. The trees were, beautiful. But so was. The city."

"We've all been more or less living off Outworld creativity for years now."

"A beautiful thing. It can take much . . . use?"

I supposed so, and we sat quietly as she watched the people, her eyes still and solemn, her head tilted. I felt if I spoke I would be intruding, and it was she who finally said: "The people. They are, beautiful also."

"Where are you from, Rhea?" I asked after watching her a while. She turned back to me.

"Byzantium." She set her eyes to the ceiling and warbled her delight at the name. "It is from, an old poem. The linguist aboard the Wagon. The first Wagon. He was, something of a poet. Our cities took, his fancy, he remembered this poem. He too was. Of Earth."

"I'm afraid I don't know the poem."

"It is, much. Old. Cities they are hammered of gold and set, in the land. All is. Beautiful there, and timeless. The poem has become for us. A song, one of our songs."

"And is your world like that? A refuge?"

"Perhaps. It was."

"Why did you leave?"

"I am going, to Ginh. To . . . work." She moved gently, looked around. I noticed again the tension in her face and hands, so unlike the easy grace of her body.

"You have a job there."

"Yes. I—" The mood passed. Her feathers rustled as she laughed: "Guess."

I declined.

"I sing." She trilled an example. Then stopped, smiling. We ordered new drinks, selecting one by name—a name she delighted in, repeating it over and over in different keys. It turned out to be a liqueur, light on the tongue, pulpy and sweet.

She leaned across the table and whispered, "It is. Nice." Her breath smelled like new-cut grass, like caramel and sea-breeze. Long plumes swept the tabletop and whispered there too. "Like the other, was."

"What do you sing, Rhea?"

"Old songs, our old songs. Of warriors. Lovers. I change the names, to theirs."

"How long will you be on Ginh?"

"Always."

You have been there before, then? No.

You have a family there? No.

You love Byzantium, you were happy there? Yes.

Then why . . . ?

"I am . . . bought. By one of the Academies. I am taken there. To sing, for them. And to be, looked at." She seemed not at all sad.

"You will miss Byzantium?"

"Yes. Much."

I cleared my throat. "Slavery is against Regulations. You——"

"It is. By my own, my will."

A long pause. . . .

I see.

"My race is. Dying. We have no techknowledgy, we are not, inUnion. Byzantium can not longer, support us. The money, they give for me. It feeds us for many years. It too buys machines. The machines will keep us. A part of us, alive."

She drew her knees up into a bower of arms and dropped her head, making the booth a nest. After a moment she lifted her face out from the feathers. She trilled, then talked.

"When I was a child, Byzantium was, quiet and still. Life it was easy. We sang our songs, made our nests, that is enough. For a lifetime, all our lives, lifetimes. That is enough. Now it is not longer easy."

"Perhaps it seemed that way. *Because* you were a child."

An arm hovered over the table. A hand came down to perch on the little round glass. "We took from her, Byzantium, she asked nothing. Our songs, our love. Not more. Our fires, to keep her, warm. The sky the earth it was. In, our homes."

"But you grew up."

"Yes and Byzantium, much old, she grows. Old-more than my Parent. Once it sang, with us. Now its voice broke, too went away. The souls left, the trees. Our homes. The rivers it swelled with sorrow, too burst. It fell, fruits from, the trees, too they were. Already dead. The moons grow red, red like the eye. Of a much old man."

"You tell it like a poem."

"It is, one of our songs. The last poem of, RoNan. He died before it was. Finished."

"Of a broken heart."

She laughed. Gently. "At the hands of, his sons. For to resist coalition. He spoke out in his songs, against the visitors. He thought, it was right, Byzantium to die. It should not be made to go on to live; living. He wanted the visitors, to leave us."

"The visitors . . . Outworld?"

She nodded. The plumes danced, so deep a blue. So deep.

"They came and to take our fruits, too our trees. They could make them to grow again-new on Ginh. They took our singers. They . . . bought, our cities, our unused nests. Then they to say, With these can you to build a new world. RoNan did not want, a new world, it would be much wrong, to Byzantium."

"And no one listened."

"They listened. Much of, them. The younger ones to not, who wanted too a life, a life of their own, a world for it. They learned, about the machines. They go much to Ginh and learned in, the Academies, there, they came back, to us. To build their new, world. Took it of the machines, like too bottomless boxes."

"Ginh. They went to Ginh. . . ."

"Yes, where I am. Going. I am with our cities, too our trees on Ginh, in a museum, there. I sing. For the people. They to come. To look at us, to listen, to me."

The ceiling speaker cleared its throat. I looked up. Nothing more.

"He must have been a strong man," I said. "To stand up so strongly for what he believed was right. To hold to it so dearly. A difficult thing to do, these days."

"The decision was not his. He had, no choice. He was, what he believed. He could not go against it."

"And so were the others, the younger ones, and they couldn't either."

"That is, the sad part."

Someone blew into the speakers.

"You knew him, you believe what he said?"

"Does it matter? He was. My father."

And we were assaulted by sound:

ATTENTION PLEASE. ATTENTION PLEASE. THE CHELTA, UNION SHIP GEE-FORTY-SEVEN, BOUND OUT, IS NOW ON PAD AND WILL LIFT IN ONE HOUR STANDARD. PASSENGERS PLEASE REPORT AT ONCE TO UNDERWAY F. UNDERWAY F.

So the strike was over, the workers would get their Pits. A pause then, some mumbled words, a shuffling of papers:

WILL CAPTAIN I-PRANH PLEASE REPORT TO THE TOWERMAIN. CAPTAIN I-PRANH TO THE TOWERMAIN. THE REVISED CHARTS HAVE BEEN COMPLETED.

And the first announcement began again.

Rhea uncurled and looked up, then back past me, as if remembering something.

Her face turned up as he approached.

"Hello, Karl," she sang. "This is, Lant." My Outworld dandy. I reached over and opened the dampers.

He bowed and smiled softly. "Pleased, Lant." Then added: "Earth, isn't it?"—seeing through my Vegan veneer as easily as he'd made out her words through the dampers. His own voice was low and full, serene. "Always pleased to meet a Terran. So few of you get out this far. But I'm afraid I'll have to be rude and take Rhea away now. That was the call for our ship. Excuse us, please."

He put out a white hand, bowing again, and she took it,

standing. Feathers rustled: a sound I would always remember.

"Thank you for talking to Rhea, Lant. I'm sure it was a great pleasure for her."

"For me."

A final bow and he turned toward the door. She stood there a moment, watching me, feathers lifting as she breathed.

"Thank you for, the drinks Lant. And for . . . to listen." She smiled. "You are going, Out. You will be on this ship. Perhaps I will. See you, on the ship."

She wouldn't, of course.

And she went away.

Most of the rest you know.

I Jumped the next day for Altar, where I got down on my calloused knees and went through my bag of time-honored politician tricks. Money bandaged the wounds of insult, outrage was salved by a new trade agreement. The Altarians would withdraw troops from Mersy: the wars were stayed.

But not stopped. The Altarians kept their sores and when, several weeks later, one of our writers published a satirical poem attacking Altar for its "weasel colonialism, that works like a vine," the wound festered open. The poet refused to apologize. He was imprisoned and properly disgraced, but the damage was done.

War erupted. Which you don't need to be told: look out your window and see the scars.

War flashed across the skies, burst inside homes. Which doesn't matter: look in your mirror for the marks that tell, the signs that stay.

I don't have to tell you that the Vegans, victims of too much sharing and always our friends, sided with us. That they were too close to the Altar allies. That they were surrounded and virtually destroyed before our ships could make the Jump.

I don't have to tell you that we're still picking up the pieces. Look out your window, look in your mirror.

That we have the bones of Union and we're trying to fatten them up again. . . .

I was one of the sideways casualties of war. One of the face-saving (for them) disgraces (for me). I believe I would have left anyway, I might have. Because there's something I have to say. And here I can say it, and be heard.

The Union gives a lot. But it takes a lot too. And I'm not sure any more that what it takes, what it shoves aside, is replaceable. Maybe some things *are* unique. I know one thing is.

Which is what I tell my students.

I sit here every day and look out at all these faces. And I wonder, Will this one be a Courier, or that one in the front row, or the one in back—the girl who swings her leg, the kid who brings sandwiches to class in his briefcase? Will they be the disciples of Earth's ascendance?

I wonder.

And I tell them that a society feeds off its people. That the larger it is, the more it consumes. That you never know what effect your words will have a hundred million miles away.

You never know. But you try. You try to know, you try to balance things out on your own scales. Utility; the best for the most; compromise and surrender. Your smallest weights are a million, a billion, people.

But I tell them something else to go with that.

I tell them . . .

That there may be nothing new under the sun. But there *are* new suns, and new faces under them. Looking up, looking down. . . .

The faces are what matter.

The little animal went racing up the side of its cage, made a leap to the top, climbed upside-down halfway out— then dropped back onto the floor. It did this over and over, steadily tumbling, becoming each time wilder, more frantic. The last time, it lay still on its back in the litter, panting.

And she was lovely below him, beside him, above him. Was lovely in dark, lovely in shadow, lovely in the glaring door as she fingered the bathroom's light. . . .

(She is sitting on the bed, legs crossed, one elbow cocked on a knee, holding a ruby fang that bites again, again into the dark around her. The window is a black hole punched in the room, and for a moment now when she lifts her arm, light slants in and falls across her belly, sparkling on semen like dew in dark grass; one breast moves against the moving arm.

Light comes again, goes again. It strikes one side of her tilted face and falls away, shadows the other. She looks down, looks up, the small motion goes along her body, her side moves against yours. There are two paths of glowing where light touched her skin, here on her belly, here on the side of her face, a dull glowing orange. Already it is fading.

Her cigarette drops through the window like a burning insect, drops into darkness. It's this kind of darkness: it can fill a room.)

She came back and sat on the edge of the bed. The light was off, her skin glowing softly orange all over, darker orange for month-old bruises on her breasts and hips. "Strong. He hadn't been with a woman for three years," she had said when he touched one of the bruises. "A real man." He had beaten her severely, then left twice what was necessary.

She struck a match and the spurt of light spiderwebbed the dirty, peeling wall.

"You're really from Earth. . . ." (Silence breaking, making sounds. The little animal moving slowly now in his cage.)

"Naturalized. During the Wars."

"Oh. I see." She was thinking about ruin, the way it started, the roads it took. Her skin was losing its glow. "Where were you born?"

"Here. Vega." (She turned to look at him.)

"In Thule." (She waited.)

"West Sector."

She turned back to the window. "I see."

"I was signed Out. It was a Vegan ship, we were getting the declaration broadcast when communication from Vega stopped. Captain turned us around but before we hit Drive, Earth told us it was too late. We went on into Drive and stayed in till we could find out what happened —Altar had ships jumping in and out all along the rim, grabbing whatever they could, blasting the rest—a big

Wagon like *The Tide* was no match for what they had. We came out near Earth. Captain's decision, and I don't envy his having to make it. Anyway, the ship was consigned and the Captain pledged to Earth. Most of us went along, enlisted. There wasn't much to come back to."

The room was quiet then with the sound of her breathing, the rustle of the animal in its litter. Light from outside crept across the floor, touching her leg on the bed with its palm. She sucked at the cigarette and its fire glowed against her face, against the window.

"You're not Terran. I thought you were."

"I'm sorry. I'm sorry I didn't tell you. I didn't realize—"

"It doesn't matter."

"But I didn't mean to——"

"It doesn't matter." She smiled. "Really."

He lay watching her face above him, a quiet face, still. And the room itself was quiet again, was gray, was graying, was dark. . . .

And later: her hand on his shoulder, her lips lightly against his and his eyes opening, something warm for his hand.

"I made coffee. You'll have to drink it black."

He stared at the cup, breathed steam and came more awake. The cup was blue ceramic, rounded, shaped into an owl's head. The eyes extended out at the edges to form handles. "You shouldn't have. Coffee's hard to get, I know, you sh——"

"I wanted to. You gave me cigarettes, I gave you coffee." She tore her cigarette in two, threw the smoking half-inch out the window, dropped the rest into the cage. Her fingers glowed orange where the cigarette had been.

"Thank you. For the coffee," he said. Then: "You're beautiful."

She smiled. "You don't have to say that."

"I wanted to."

And she laughed, at that.

He got up and walked to the cage, his hands wrapped around the mug. The little animal was leaning down on its front legs, hindquarters up, paws calmly working at the cigarette. It had carefully slit the paper and was removing the tiny lumps of charcoal from the filter one at a time, putting them in its mouth.

"Charcoal," she said. "There's charcoal in the filter, I just remembered. He likes it."

Having finished eating, the little animal rolled the remaining paper into a ball, carried it to one corner and deposited it there. Then it returned to the front of the cage and sat licking at the orange fur that tufted out around its paws.

"What is it?" he asked after a while. The charcoal pellets were still in its mouth. After sucking at them for several moments, it began to grind them between its teeth.

"A Veltdan."

"Vegan?"

She nodded.

"I've never seen one."

"There aren't many left—none around the cities. Dying out. They're from Larne Valley."

He thought a moment, remembered: "The telepaths!" The colony of misanthropic sensitives.

"Yes. That's where the colony is. I was born there, came to Kahlu after the Wars. Not much left, even that far out.

The colony was wiped out."

"Are you——"

She shook her head. "My mother. Mostly I was born without their physical deformity or their talents, though I guess I got a *little* of both." She came up to the cage, thumped her fingers against the side. "The telepathy . . . some of it filtered down. I'm an empathist, of sorts." She grinned. "Makes me good at my work."

She walked to the bed and lit another cigarette. An insect came in through the window, skittered around the room hitting the ceiling again and again, finally found the window and flew back out. It was neon, electric blue.

"Veltdans are supposed to be the deadliest things in the universe. Four inches from nose to tail, altogether seven pounds—and you can put them up against any animal you want to, any size, any weight."

He took his hand off the cage and put it back around the mug. The Veltdan was over on its back in the litter, rolling from side to side, square snout making arcs. Watching this prim, almost exquisite little animal, he found it difficult to accept what she was saying; to put the two facts together.

"It registers external emotion. Whatever made the telepaths got into the Veltdan too—as much as they can handle with their brain. You get something coming at it with a mind full of hate and killing, the Veltdan takes it all and turns it back on the attacker—goes into a frenzy, swarms all over it, knows what the attacker is going to do next. It's small but it's fast, it has sharp claws and teeth. While the attacker is getting filled back up with its own hate and fury, the Veltdan is tearing it to pieces. They say two of them fighting each other is really something to see, it just goes on and on."

He looked down at the little orange-cerulean animal. "Why should they fight one another?"

"Because that's what they like best to eat: each other."

He grimaced and walked to the window. A shuttleship was lifting. Its light flashed against his face.

Every day just past noon, flat clouds gather like lily pads in the sky, float together, rain hops off to pound on the ground. For an hour the rain comes down, washing the haze of orange from the air, and for that hour people come together in cafés and Catches, group there talking. And waiting.

They were sitting in an outdoor Catch, drinking coffee. Minutes before, clattering and thumping, a canvas roof had been rolled out over them. Around them now the crowd moved and talked. Rain slammed down, slapped like applause on the canvas roof.

"This is where the artists come," she said, pointing to a corner of the Catch where several young people were grouped around a small table. Two of them—a young man with his head shaved and a girl with long ochre hair —were bent forward out over the table, talking excitedly. The others were listening closely, offering occasional comments. When this happened the young man would tilt his head away from the speaker and watch him closely; the girl would look down at the floor, a distant expression on her face. Then when the speaker had finished they would look at one another and somehow, silently, they would decide: one of them would reply. Cups, saucers, crumpled sheets of paper were piled on the table. One of the girls was sketching. Rain sprinkled and splattered on the backs of those nearest the outside.

"The one talking, that's Dave," she went on. "A ceramist, and some say he's the best in Union. I have a few of his pots at home. Early stuff, functional. He used to do a lot of owls; everything he threw had an owl in it. Now he's on olms. Salamanders. They're transparent, live in caves. If you take one out into the sun it burns. Turns black and dies." She lit one of the cigarettes he'd given her. "They all come here every afternoon. Some work at night, some just wait for the next afternoon. I have a lot of their work." She seemed quite proud of that.

"You like art quite a lot, then?"

"No." She grinned, apologizing. "I don't even understand most of it. But I seem to feel it—what they think, their appreciation. And I like them, the people. They always need money, too."

She sat quietly for a moment, smoking, watching the group of young people.

"It's a tradition, coming here. This Catch was built where the *Old Union* was before the Wars; Samthar Smith always came here when he was on Vega. It's called *Pergamum* now."

" 'All Pergamum is covered with thorn bushes; even its ruins have perished.' The epigraph for his novel, *Pergamum*. The eulogy he wrote for his marriage."

"Yes." She stared out at the rain. "I love that book." Then she looked back at him. "Dave tells me they've taken the name as a symbol. The ruin of the old, the growth of a new art."

A disturbance near the center of the Catch caught his attention. Holding a glass of punjil, a fat middle-aged man was struggling to his feet while the others at his table tried to get him to sit back down. He brushed aside their hands and remarks, came swaying and grinning across the floor. Halfway across, he turned around and went back to put his drink on the table, spilling it as he did so.

"Hi," he said, approaching the table, then belched. "Thought I'd come over and say that—Hi, I mean. C'n always spot a fellow Terran." Another belch. "William Beck Mann, representing United Union Travel, glad to meet you." He leaned on the table with one hand, shoved the other out across it. "Coming in from Ginh, stuck on this goddamn dead rock while the com'pny ship gets its charts revised or somethin'. Nothing going on here at all, eh. You heading home too?"

Others in the Catch, Vegans, were staring toward their table in distaste.

"No . . . I don't know. Maybe."

"Mind if I sit 'own?" Which he did, swiveling on the tabled hand, plopping into the chair.

"No, I don't mind. But we're about to leave."

"I see." He looked at the girl for the first time and grinned. His teeth were yellow. "Guess you got plans. Well. That case, s'pose I'll get on back." The fat man hauled himself out of the chair and went back toward his own table. Two of the young people were leaving and he tried to walk between them, knocking the girl against a table. Hatred flared in the boy's face and a knife suddenly appeared in his hand.

"No, Terri, don't," the girl said. "He's drunk, he can't help himself."

The boy reached and pulled her to him. Then, just as suddenly as it had come, the hatred vanished from his face. He smiled squarely into the man's face (the knife, too, had vanished) and spat at him. He and the girl went on out of the Catch, holding hands. The fat man goggled after them, reeling out obscenities till someone from his table came and took him back.

"You know which part I like best?" she said after a while. "In *Pergamum?*" She turned from the rain and looked at him. "The part where the girl pours coffee and says, 'This is the universe.' Then she holds up two rocks of sugar and says, 'And this is us, the two of us.' She drops the sugar in the coffee and it starts dissolving, you can't see it any more. . . ."

"Yes, I know. They say it really happened, that Smith heard of it from one of his friends and later used it in *Pergamum*. I wonder if the friend felt honored?"

"I would have. He was a great man."

"He was also a very lonely man."

Disheartedly, they began to argue over whether Smith should be called a Terran or Vegan poet. She seemed strangely affected by the previous trouble, and his heart was just not in the discussion. Smith had been born on Earth, had adopted Vega as his home for many years. . . .

She had difficulty lighting her next cigarette. The rain was over and the winds were rising now.

A shuttleship was lifting.

Against the darkness, bands of pearl spread in layers and deepened, swelling into rainbow colors. They flashed on his face. When he turned from the window, her skin was glowing rich orange.

"Will you stay here? Have you come home now?"

"I don't know. That's why I came. To find out."

"It would be nice. If you stayed." She fed the Veltdan another filter; it was making muted, moaning sounds. "That's one of Dave's cups," she said. "He also built the cage for me."

Everything was quiet for a long while.

Finally he said: "Do you remember how *Pergamum* ends?"

" 'Wherever we are content, that is our country.' "

He nodded. "That's what I have to decide. Where I'm content, where my country is." He put the cup on the cage. "We keep talking about Samthar Smith. . . ."

"An Earthman who became Vegan, as you're a Vegan who became Terran."

He turned to look at her. The orange glow was fading. He nodded again. "He finally found contentment. On Juhlz."

"And you?"

He shrugged. The Veltdan was grinding the tiny bits of charcoal between its teeth. It sounded like someone walking over seashells far away.

"There's an insect. On Earth," he said. "It dies when you pick it up. From the heat in your hand." He walked toward the bathroom.

A moment later: "The switch isn't working."

"There's a power ration. This area's cut off for several hours, another gets to use the power. The peak periods are shifted about."

He came back and stared sadly at her.

"You don't know how ridiculous that is, do you? You don't realize. There's enough power on my ship—on one goddamn ship!—to give Vega electricity for years. You don't see how absurd that is, do you? You just accept it." He picked up the cup. The Veltdan was carrying its rolled-up paper toward the corner of the cage.

Suddenly he threw the cup across the room. It struck the wall and shattered; one eye-handle slid back across the floor and lay at his feet, staring up at him.

"I'm sorry," he said.

"It doesn't matter. I can get another from Dave. An olm, one of his olms."

"I'll leave you money."

"It doesn't matter." She bent and began picking up the shards. "Besides, I have others. Would you like more coffee? Now?"

"No . . . thank you." He walked back to the window and stood there for several minutes, staring out. He could hear the Veltdan pacing in its cage.

"You know," he said finally, "I feel free now. Because of you, and all this. I feel free, content. I can go on."

When she spoke, her voice was very quiet. "Then you're not staying."

He paused. "No."

Then: "Thank you, thank you very much. I'll leave money . . . for the cup."

She turned away from him, and spoke very softly again. "It doesn't matter." The Veltdan depended from the top of the cage. "I knew you would, from the first. You never believed you would stay. I could tell." She sighed. "The empathy."

He took the blue shards out of her hands and put them in the empty waste-bucket. Then he put money on the cage and left.

Pearl spread outward and shelled the sky.

She stood at the window watching. The colors deepened, flared to a rainbow. Her skin glowed orange under the colors; the cigarette in her hand gleamed weakly.

Behind her the little Veltdan sat very still in its cage and blinked at the light.

The Opening of the
Terran Ballet*

Barii Volk is of course Jordon Ligochee's son. Just ten
years after Jordon's publication of his five-page *Design for
Loving* established him as our finest contemporary poet,
sixteen-year-old Barii echoed his father's success with
Shadows, a collection of lyrics ("antiques") in the de-
manding Rilkash stress-control manner. It was, however,
to prove more than an echo. The shadows were to pass
under relentless examination and Barii was to carry his
lyricism and formalism to its logical, though unantici-
pated, limits; besides his *Floors of My Heart*, the next
year saw a number of uniquely instrumented chamber

* Reprinted from: *The Lyric Quarterly*, Vol. 9, No. 2, 2465

works and the debut of his *First Symphony* (*The Whi-lom*), played by the New Union Ensemble and conducted by the young composer himself, who came to the console rather like a skinny bird and departed it, after the final drawn beat of his baton and the hammer-blows of thundering ovation, in a heap of sweaty clothing, his hair unkempt, his face drained and weak—happy with the reception afforded this return of his to ancient forms.

In months to come, though, Barii was to move on to newer forms of expression; indeed, one critic remarked that Barii Volk was by himself encompassing the full range and development of contemporary art media. He was to pioneer in the growth of sound crystals, work that finally resulted in the delicately beautiful *Mauve Neck-lace* now housed at the Kahlu Museum, sprinkling out impromptu sonatas as the light strikes it, molding its tones and structure to the shifting patterns of light in the room and to the movement of viewers. He was to be one of the first to experiment with energy sculpture, the best-known example of his work being the *Waiting Room* commissioned by Councilhome; walking through it, one experiences every neural nuance of anxiety and anticipation. He was to introduce the fraloom to Larnian music and train young performers in the technique of this many-voiced instrument. Everything he took up seemed transformed; critics remarked his insight into essential structures. We all waited to see where his interests would next fall.

And then, five years ago, came the startling news of his renunciation of Larne citizenship. Barii was not available for comment, and for evidence or explanation we had only three poems published a month later—anonymously, yet bearing the unmistakable stamp of Barii's lyricism.

One was in French, that strange ancestor of our own language; the others were translations, one from the Rilkash, one from ancient Anglaise. . . .

> *jamais revoir face à vous dans la glace*
> *en arrière de moi*
> *où dans les ans nous trouvons content*
> *à nous*

> The tree goes on
> Into the sky; branch, leaf, twig

> Do not stop it.

> One lifts
> a foot, and puts another
> in front of it
> to claim

> the generous sky.

Some time later, a small privately printed volume made its appearance. Entitled *Occasion:Départ*, it consisted of a number of extremely short, inter-related "fragments," or units of poetic occasion (the occasion of a single moment, arrested in time). The theme was that of "Coincidence/Collision: the form of a life, the fact of a world perceived." (From the Preface.) There was great disputation among scholars as to whether the piece could actually be considered a single, integrated *moment*, that is, a poem; or if it must finally be seen as nothing more than a collection of fragments, notes *for* poems. (I trust that I have made clear my own position on this matter, both here and in several earlier monographs which were in fact among the first studies effected.) Also, there was considerable debate over the volume's intentions and significance—what, for instance, was one to make of the glim-

mers of another of our ancient languages, Polish? (I refer
the reader to my book *Orthographies* for further illumina-
tion in this regard, in particular to its thesis of the generation of our language—whose origins I find most manifest
in Polish and, of course, French.) Suffice it to say, then,
that the reaction was mixed: there were even those who
held it to be the literary hoax of the century. At any rate,
though the poems appear for the most part translations
from "English," and are indeed contingent to the three
earlier poems both in substance and structure, most au-
thorities yet agree that there is insufficient evidence to
attribute them incontrovertibly to Barii. I believe a few
examples should therefore be in order. (Unfortunately
space, in the confines of this piece at hand, is limited.
Those further interested might look to my essay "Event &
Advent," reprinted in *Orthographies.*)

> That tree would ascend to the sky.
> And your hand
> On the trunk grown larger.

> puste płótno, cień żagli,
> ruch rosypanych pomysłów;
> i podpalam powrotne kroki
> jest nowy obrót twórcych sił.

> Whatever you wanted remains
> Behind; still, there are paths
> You didn't follow.

> *où fus-tu où je toi voulais je suis*
> *dans la foncé du jour seul*

For months, then, nothing was heard from the eight-
een-year-old poet; no amount of inquiry, however in-

trepid, however privileged, could discover any clue as to his whereabouts or current activities. Later we learned he had left the planet. Shortly after, Jordon Ligochee, who had been deeply hurt by his son's action, died.

Four years passed. Gradually rumors began: Barii had left Union, had left the system, had gone to Earth. We all smiled at the image of young Barii there on our dark exhausted world, little believing that it could be true, that he was there, so far away, working among those empty defeated people. At which point the announcements arrived, each one personally signed by Barii Volk and posted from Earth.

It is rumored that the Director of the Council of Arts, upon receiving his invitation, responded: "What the hell is a ballet?" (It is also rumored that he responded: "Where the hell is Earth?" But I believe we may safely put that down as apocryphal.) Perhaps so. At any rate, the response communicated, as well, his intention to attend.

In due course I received my own invitation and secured passage on one of the Earthbound wagons. At the suggestion of this magazine's editor I approached Barii for an interview, which, to our mutual surprise, was granted, it being arranged that I should meet him at the theatre in New Rome upon my arrival; this was to be the afternoon before the first performance of his ballet.

I found him just off the heart of the theatre, in a small room crowded with books and unfamiliar musical instruments. He was slumping on a couch, bent over a large six-stringed instrument, performing some minor adjustment while another, much older man—doubtless the musician—stood by waiting. Barii had put on weight in the past years, come to resemble less the skinny bird with which I'd always compared him. Also, he had abandoned his familiar flamboyance of dress and was now attired in the plain, rough clothing I'd noticed on others about the theatre; but when, moments later, he looked up, I perceived again those familiar dark eyes, the sharp face, that quick and slightly mocking smile. His hair was gathered with a ribbon to one side of his head.

He must have heard my approach for, just as I lifted my hand to knock at the doorsill, he sprang from the chair and came striding toward me across the room. "James? I've followed your work with a great deal of interest and admiration. Your article on Arndto I found particularly helpful . . . and your own *Third Cycle*, of course. I'm pleased to meet you at last; in fact, anticipation of that pleasure was the reason I responded so happily to your note about an interview."

I must admit that I was a bit surprised at his familiarity with my work, and with the esteem he afforded these small contributions of mine. I smiled and said, "I thought you should like the opportunity to talk about your new work, after these many years of silence."

"I would prefer to let the ballet speak for itself." He turned and held the instrument out to the waiting man: "Here, John, I think that should take care of it. If there's any further trouble, bring it back." The man came across the room and took the instrument. "John, this is James Sallis. He's come from Larne for our little performance. James—my concertmaster, John Bramin."

My face must have betrayed my mystery at the term,

for Barii quickly smiled and explained: "The concertmaster is the first violin. The most important single member of the orchestra."

The man tucked the instrument under his arm, grinned, and walked away in a slow, stooping gait. Several others met him just outside the door and they walked off together, chattering. Something which had registered subliminally long ago suddenly sprang to the front of my mind: that Barii, like the people here, was noticeably shorter than the rest of us.

"Please sit," Barii said. "And perhaps you would like to try some beer." He crossed to a shelf and brought back a large jar, the top of which he unscrewed and put aside, handing the jar over to me. It was half-filled with a yellow-brown liquid in which light swam and rolled. "Don't worry, it's quite sanitary. I produce it myself, in small quantities. That extra space is necessary to obtain full body and flavor: it should be just about right, now."

I accepted the jar and drank (the world was sudden, amber, in the brass-bright depths). It was heavy—fluid rather than liquid—with a sweet but somehow quite satisfying taste. I expressed my approval.

"I don't think I have it *quite* right yet, but it *is* refreshing, isn't it? One of the small pleasures we lost when we gave Earth up for dead."

We sat for several minutes talking of Larne and what the younger artists were engaged in there. I told Barii about the new odor symphonies, which owed so much to his early work, and spoke to him of Heinreid Flant, who seems to me the most brilliant and inspired of the new generation of energy sculptors. Barii inquired briefly about microsculpture, something with which he professed he had always wanted to work yet had never found the opportunity. "The journals always give a prejudiced view of what's really going on," he remarked, then flashed a grin, remembering the auspices under which I'd initially approached him.

"You called that instrument a violin," I finally asked. "Would you care to tell me more about it?"

For the next hour or so I was offered up what must surely be one of the most comprehensive surveys of musical history existent. Barii told me how he had traced the evolution of our own instruments backwards to the ones I would see utilized in the ballet later that night; how he had been forced to reconstruct the peculiar musical scale of ancient Earth then, from books and the memory of a few of the older Terrans, reconstruct the instruments around those concepts. "I have undoubtedly made many mistakes," he said at one point. "The violin for instance: should it have six strings tuned E–A–D–G–B–E, or four tuned E–A–D–G? I finally settled on six."

There was a light knock at the door and Barii sprang to his feet. It was a girl.

"Barii, I'm sorry to bother you, but there's a problem in the score. Movement Seven. The choreography and accompaniment are a little out of synch."

Barii took her hand and led her into the room. She was very young, smaller even than Barii, her hair short and colorless. She had huge green eyes. "Nonsense, Verity, you mustn't be always apologizing. James: my leading lady, Verity. James Sallis, from *Lyric Quarterly*. On Larne." She smiled and he squeezed her hand gently, turning her toward the door. "I'll be with you in a few minutes, darling. You mustn't worry, everything will be all right."

She left, looking sadly down at the floor, and Barii

continued his explanation, much of which I have reported in the second part of the present article. Frequently people came to the door with last-minute troubles and were politely turned away with assurances that he would be along soon, "they musn't worry." It was almost as though they resented, or were deeply saddened by my taking Barii away from them, even for a few moments. I kept trying to steer our conversation toward the ballet itself but Barii resisted every attempt, mentioning only that the work was dedicated to his father.

Even when he had reconstructed the scale and instruments, he went on, his work was far from finished. He had then to learn the Terran language perfectly ("It is incredibly idiosyncratic"); to make a deep study of Earth myth and legend; and to train his performers—to make artists of a people who had sunk to a virtually pre-agricultural society. "I saw it as a moving outward," he intimated, "by returning to origins. I felt, I was sure, that a vitality existed here—a vitality I needed, and could make much use of. In the course of my study I discovered the ballet and I felt that here was the perfect medium for me: at once personal and formal. A pure lyricism, combining myth and language and music and motion . . . plus a rigorous form. It was the end of all my previous work and, at the same time, possessed everything which that previous work had lacked."

He waved aside my objection to that final remark.

"I'm sorry, I just felt closed in. That I had exhausted the possibilities. This may have been the explanation for my peripatetic courting of artistic forms toward the end, before I left Larne. At least, that was my final decision, and I tried to make it clear in some translations I published anonymously. I was looking for something which I could never have found, something which no longer existed there. Here, I think, I found it."

Our conversation continued for some minutes, but I could get Barii to say no more about the ballet. Eventually I could see that he was tiring of our talk—becoming anxious to get out among his musicians—and excused myself, again expressing my anticipation of the performance which would be commencing in a few hours' time now.

Barii stood and shook the hair back away from his face. He took my hands between his own.

"It's been truly wonderful to meet you, James," he said, looking into my eyes. "I hope you'll not be too terribly disappointed with our little ballet. I really hope that. . . . Good-bye."

I took my leave and walked on the hills above the theatre to wait for the performance.

The sky was gray, impending, with streams of ochre and maroon on the horizon. Leaves like the husks of sigflees on Larne covered the hills, and I dimly understood that this was somehow the result of the "seasons" which Barii had mentioned in our conversation, though I found the concept basically impenetrable. Wind tumbled in the leaves as I walked among them. They crunched beneath my feet.

The ballet was titled *Jordon,* and was dedicated to Barii's father. Would it achieve that union of lyricism and formalism he hoped for? Had he found an answer to the exhaustion of our forms, found the vitality he wanted—or was his love for this world and its people blinding him, obscuring his critical senses, causing him to delude himself and accept mediocrity as vital? There had been clues, certain words in his conversation, certain gestures, which could indicate his awareness of the ballet's failure. But he placed great faith in it, had devoted to it so many years of his life. . . .

These were the thoughts that crowded my mind as I walked alone on the hill through the leaves, all scarlet and mud-brown. The streams of color on the horizon were flattening, disappearing. There was a sense of dampness in the air and in my lungs, too, as I breathed.

I sat on the stump of a tree and looked down at the ramshackle theatre far below. As I watched, two tiny figures came out and looked up toward me. One raised his hand and waved; the other hesitated a moment then waved as well. They started off together away from the theatre and from me, holding hands.

The darkness, the dampness, was drawing closer around me. I sat on the hill for several minutes more, then went down to wait with the others for the opening of the ballet.

The History Makers

In the morning (he wasn't sure which morning) he began
the letter. . . .

Dear Jim,

      The last time I saw you, you advised
against my coming here. You were quite insistent, and I
don't believe the perfectly awful 3–2 beer we were drinking was wholly responsible for said adamance. You virtually begged me not to come. And I suppose you must
have felt somewhat duty-bound to sway me away. That
since it was yourself who introduced me to the Ephemera,

you'd incurred some sort of liability for my Fate. That you would be accountable.

I remember you said a man couldn't keep his sanity here; that his mind would be whirled in a hundred directions at once, and he would ravel to loose ends—that he would crimp and crumble, swell and burst, along with this world. And you held that there was nothing of value here. But the government and I, for our separate reasons, disagreed.

And can I refute you now by saying that I've found peace, or purpose, or insight? No, of course not, not in or with this letter. For all my whilom grandiloquence, and accustomed to it as you are, such an effort would be fatuous and absurd. What I *can* do: I can show you this world in what is possibly the only way we can ever know it, I can show you where it brims over to touch my own edges. I can let you look out my window.

The Blue Twin. That was . . . three years ago? Close to that. ("Time is merely a device to keep everything from happening at once." Isn't that wonderful? I found it in one of the magazines I brought out with me, in a review of some artist's work about which I remember only the name of one painting: A Romantic Longing to Be Scientific.) Three years . . . I miss Earth, dark Earth. I miss Vega.

(I remember that you were shortly to be reassigned to Ginh, and wonder if this letter will find you there among the towers.)

The Blue Twin, which we always insisted was the best bar in the Combine at least, probably the Union (and did I ever tell you that bars are the emblem of our civilization? A place to lean back in, to put your feet up, a place of silences and lurching conversations: still center, hub for a whirling universe. And pardon my euphuism, please).

And the two of us sitting there, talking of careers and things. Quietly, with the color-clustered walls of sky-bright Vega around us and the massive turning shut out. You dissuading. And bits of my land slaking into the sea. Talking, taking time to talk.

My work had soured, yours burgeoned, I envied you (though we always pretended it was the other way around). All my faces had run together like cheap water-color. My classes had come to be for me nothing but abstract patterns, forming, breaking, reforming—while the faces around you were becoming distinct, defining themselves, giving you ways to go.

I envied you. So I took this sabbatical: "to do a book." And the sabbatical became an extended leave of absence, and that became a dismissal. And no book.

Things fall apart, the center cannot hold. . . . Talking about dissent and resolution, the ways of change, things falling by the way and no Samaritan—and you mention-ing something you'd seen in one of the Courier bulletins that crossed your desk: which was my introduction to it all, to Ephemera. (Ephemera. It was one of those pale poetic jokes, the sort that gave us Byzantium and Eldo-rado and Limbo and all the others, names for out-Union planets, for distant places. You wonder what kind of man is responsible.)

How many weeks then of reading, of requesting infor-mation, of clotted first drafts? How long before the night I collapsed into my bed and sat up again with the line "Hold hard these ancient minutes in a cuckoo's month" on my lips—days, weeks? It seemed years. Time, for me, had broken down. And I came to Ephemera. . . .

The Ephemera. My window looks out now on one of their major cities, towered and splendid, the one I've come to call Siva. It is middle season, which means they are expanding: yesterday the city was miles away, a dark line on the horizon; tomorrow it will draw even closer and I'll have to move my squatter's-hut back out of the way. The next day it will swell toward me again, then in the afternoon retreat—and the collapse will have begun. By the next morning I'll be able to see nothing of Siva, and the hut will have to be relocated, shuttled back in for the final moments.

They live in a separate time-plane from ours—is that too abrupt? I don't know another way to say it, or how I should prepare for saying it. Or even if it makes sense. They are but vaguely aware of my presence, and I can study them only with the extensive aid of machines, some I brought with me, a few I was able to requisition later (the government always hopes, always holds on to a chance for new resources). And all I've learned comes down to that one strange phrase. A separate time-plane.

When I first came here, I was constantly blundering into the edges of their city, or being blundered into by them; I was constantly making hasty retreats back into what I started calling the Deadlands. It took my first year just to plot the course of the cities. I've gotten little further.

It's a simple thing, once you have the key: the cities develop in dependence to the seasons. The problem comes with Ephemera's orbit, which is wildly eccentric (I'm tempted to say erratic), and with her queer climate. Seasons flash by, repeat themselves with subtle differences, linger and rush—all in apparent confusion. It takes a while to sort it all out in your mind, to resolve a year into particulars.

And now I've watched this city with its thousand names surge and subside a thousand times. I've watched its cycles repeat my charts, and I've thrown away the charts and been satisfied to call it Siva. All my social theories, my notes, my scribble-occluded papers, I've had to put away; I became a scientist, then simply an observer. Watching Siva.

It's always striking and beautiful. A few huts appear and before you can breathe a village is standing there. The huts sprawl out across the landscape and the whole thing begins to ripple with the changes that are going on, something as though the city were boiling. This visual undulation continues; the edges of the village move out away from it, catch the rippling, extend further: a continuous process. The farther from center, the faster it moves. There's a time you recognize it as a town, a time when the undulation slows and almost stops—then, minutes later, endogeny begins again and its growth accelerates fantastically. It sprawls, it rises, it solidifies.

(A few days ago while I was watching, I got up to put some music—it was Bach—on the recorder. Then I came back and sat down. I must have become absorbed in the music, because later when the tape cut off, I looked up and the city was almost upon me. I keep thinking that someday I won't move back, that I'll be taken into the city, it will sprout and explode around me.)

Siva builds and swells, explodes upward, outward, blankets the landscape. Then, toward the end of the cycle, a strange peace inhabits it: a pause, a silence. Like Joshua's stopping the sun.

And then: what? I can't know what goes on in the city at these times. From photographs (rather incredible photographs) and inspection of the "ruins," I've gathered that something like this must occur: some psychic shakedown hits the people in full stride; most of them go catto, fold themselves into insensible knots—while the rest turn against the city and destroy it. Each time, it happens. Each time, I'm unable to discover the respective groups or even the overall reason. And each time, destruction is absolute. The momentary stasis breaks, and the city falls away. No wall or relic is left standing; even the rubble is somehow consumed. It happens so quickly the cameras can't follow it; and I walk about for hours afterward, trying to read something in the scarred ground. . . . "All Pergamum is covered with thorn bushes; even its ruins have perished."

Three years. Amusing and frightening to think of all I've seen in that time, more than any other man. And what have I learned? One thing perhaps, one clear thing, and this by accident, poking about the "ruins." I found one of their devices for measuring time, which had inexplicably survived the relapse, a sort of recomplicated sundial—and I guessed from it that this race reckons time from conclusions rather than beginnings. (I leave it to you to decide whether this is a philosophical or psychological insight.) That is, their day—or year, or century, or whatever they might have termed it—seems to have been delimited by the sun's declension rather than its rise; and I assume this scheme, this perspective, would have become generalized (or itself simply expressed an already prevailing attitude). There's a part of the mechanism—a curious device, either rectifier or drive control, possibly both—that seems to work by the flux of the wind, I suppose bringing some sort of complex precision into their measurements: a kind of Aeolian clock.

And since that last sentence there's been a long pause as I sat here and tried to think: what can I say now. . . . Hours ago, when I began this letter, I had some vague, instinctive notion of things I wanted to tell you. Now it's all fallen back out of reach again, and all I have for you and for myself are these pages of phatic gesturing: Look. See. That, and the first piece of an epiphany, an old song from the early years of Darkearth: "Time, time is winding up again."

And so I sit here and look out my window, watching this city build and fall. I stare at their clock, which no longer functions, and have no use for my own. I am backed to the sea, and tomorrow Siva will spread and extend out onto these waters. I'm left with the decision, the ancient decision: shall I move?

I put on my music—my Bach, my Mozart, my Telemann—and I beat out its rhythms on chrome tiles. For a while I lose myself in it, for a while I break out of the gather and issue of time. . . .

And outside now, the sky fills with color like a bowl of strung ribbons, the ribbons fall, night billows about me. Twelve times I've begun this letter over a space of months, and each time faltered. Now at last, like the day, I've run through to a stammering end. I've filled hours and pages. Yet all I have to offer you is this: this record of my disability. Which I send with enduring love.

Your brother,
John

In the evening he finished the letter and set it aside and felt the drag of the sea against his chest.

He sat at the empty table he used for a desk, looking up at the opposite wall. On it, two reproductions and a mirror, forming a caret: mirror at the angle, below and left The Persistence of Memory, one of Monet's Notre Dame paintings across from that. Glass bolted in place, stiff paper tacked up—time arrested, time suspended, time recorded in passing. And about them depended the banks of shelves and instrumentation which covered the hut's walls like lines and symbols ranked on a page.

He rose, making a portrait of the mirror, seeing: this moment. Behind that, three years. Behind that, a lifetime. And behind that, nothing.

(Take for heraldry this image: the palimpsest, imperfectly erased.)

He ambled about his room, staring at the strange, three-dimensional objects which surrounded him, not understanding. He picked up the Ephemera chronometer, turned it over in his hands, put it back. Then (four steps) he stood by the tapedeck. Making sound, shaping sound.

(All of this, all so . . . vivid, so clearly defined. Clear and sharp like an abstraction of plane intersecting plane, angle and obtrusion . . . hard, sharp on a flat ground.)

Bach churned out of the speakers, rose in volume as he spun controls, rose again till bass boomed and the walls rattled.

And then he was walking on the bare gray ground outside his hut. . . .

(Feet killing quiet. No: because the silence hums like a live wire, sings like a thrown knife. Rather, my feet tick on the sands. Passing now a flat rock stood on its feet, leaning against the sky. A poem remembered. . . . Time passes, you say. No. We go; time stays. . . . And on Rhea there are a thousand vast molelike creatures burrowing away forever in heart-darkness, consuming a world.)

He stopped and stood on the beach in the baritone darkness, with the pale red sea ahead and the timed floodlights burning behind him. Three yards off, a fish broke water and sank back into a target of ripples.

Looked up. Four stars ticked in the sky, an orange moon shuttled up among them.

Looked down. The city, Siva, swept toward him.

(A simple truth. What denies time, dies. And that which accepts it, which places itself in time, lives again. Emblem of palimpsests. Vision of this palimpsest city. Saturn devouring his children.)

The Bach came to his ears then, urgent, exultant. The night was basso profundo, the moon boxed in stars. He sat watching a beetle scuttle across the sand, pushing a pebble before it, deep red on gray.

Later he looked up and the music was over. He turned and saw Siva at his penumbra's edge, turned back to still water.

Turned back to silence. . . .

Then the lights went off behind him and he was left alone with the fall and the surge of the sea.

II

And then the dark—

"Dow accepted the contract because we
think that simple good citizenship requires
that we supply our government and our
military with those goods they need when
we have the technology and the capability
and have been chosen by the government
as suppliers."

DOW, 1966

"Good evening, Mr. Davis."

He lifted his head to peer into dimness outside the
influence of his lamp. (*Two shapes, men in coats. Fog on
the window. Lights outside.*) He put down the pen;
moved his hand out across the desk, out across the leather-
framed blotter.

"No. Don't move the lamp, Mr. Davis. And I'm afraid
we'll have to ask you to keep your hands where they are.
Visible."

One of the men shut the door and stood with his back to it, eyes on the window. The other walked across the room (*in window light: tall, thin, dark eyes, pale; heels soft in the carpet*) and slumped into the padded chair. Reaching under his coat he brought out a cigarette, matches—struck a match and held it near his face (*yellow, shadows, cavernous eyes*). He leaned out across the desk to drag the ashtray toward him (*it was full; ashes spilled around it*), then sat in the chair smoking quietly.

And Davis sat staring out over a slab of white light at two men and a window.

Three o'clock. And the leaves are afraid, they tremble on the trees.

He is sitting in a dark room, a room of orange and green, smoking. Outside the window the limbs of trees move ponderously, like the legs of huge dying insects. A forgotten radio blats late news from the white-tiled kitchen.

(*How to escape this sense of the darkness, filling?*)

He hears the sound of feet on the stairs, and the door from the staircase opens into the room. "Darling. . . ." She is gray-eyed with sleep, holding a gown close against her breasts.

"I couldn't sleep."

"Again."

There is a sudden thrust of wind and one branch dips violently, scratching along the glass. He lights another cigarette and, hand shaking, reaches out toward his cup. Cold, gray coffee and grounds like tiny cinders run out across the table's mirror top.

("We'll have to put on a new shift: twenty-four hour production."

"I believe Goodrich has a breakdown on the new figures."

They all look down the table toward Goodrich, who now stands, shuffling papers, his meerschaum pipe smoking away like one of the plant's chimneys.)

She is bending down to the table. The loose skin at her stomach swings gently, showing in outline under the gown; her breasts, still enlarged, move against her arm. She stands, damp rag in one hand, cup in the other, and goes out to the kitchen; comes back with a drink.

"They've doubled the order," he tells her. Her hair is disarrayed, tangled down around her face. The gown falls just above her knees and her feet are bare, toes curled against the cold.

(*When thoughts turn sour and refuse to stick; the whole thing shatters across like struck glass.*)

"Darling. . . ."

Upstairs the baby wakes crying, frightened by the wind.

Finally: "Working late aren't you, Mr. Davis?"

"End of the year. Lot of paperwork to clear up."

The man smiled, looking over the things on Davis' desk. "But you're not working on that, are you?" He nodded toward the blotter, where Davis' arm covered a much-corrected sheet of paper. "A statement, perhaps? For the press?"

Davis started to stand and the one at the door jerked his head around to watch him. "Please sit down, Mr. Davis," the thin one said.

"Who are you? How did you get in here?"

"Sit down."

He sank into the chair. The man at the door turned his head away again, stared back at the window.

"Now, it doesn't matter who we are, does it? You remember that—just someone working late, like you. Just a visit; we just came to have a little talk with you. That's all."

"If this is a robbery, I'm afraid your timing is off. The vault's sealed for the night. And the payroll doesn't come in until tomorrow. Afternoon."

The thin one snubbed his cigarette out, pushing more ashes over the edge onto the desk. "Really, Mr. Davis, I did expect better of you." He laid his hand on the leather arm. His fingers were long and thin; they trembled slightly. "Don't make our little talk difficult, any more difficult than it has to be. Please. No need to be coy." Now Davis could make out the features of the man at the window. It was a nondescript face: chinless, balding, ordinary. He was heavy, and stood solidly on his feet, eyes on the window with (Davis suddenly thought) the attitude of a retired sergeant who, still, comes automatically to attention. Davis imagined he might be wearing combat boots, polished to a deep black shine.

"As for how," the thin one went on, "shall we just say that certain of your employees came to you with quite outstanding records and . . . recommendations." He smiled again, and the skin tightened across his face. "There won't be any record of our little visit, of course."

"I see."

The man lit another cigarette and tossed the match into the ashtray. Ashes puffed up where it hit. When he raised the cigarette to his face, Davis noticed again the odd contrast, the slackness of the man's body and the nervousness of his hands.

"Good." Blue smoke spiraled toward the ceiling, drifted into the lamp's light, from the cigarette held motionless in front of his face. "Like to talk now, Mr. Davis?" From behind the cigarette.

Davis shook his head.

Silence. Smoke.

"No? And I'd heard you had so very much to say, things you wanted to say so very urgently."

The man settled lower in the chair, put out his legs and crossed his ankles. A daub of ash fell onto the front of his coat, sparking for a moment before the tiny fire went out. He sat very still. Only his arm moved now, carrying the cigarette up to his mouth, away from his mouth, up to his mouth. . . .

Finally: "Sedition, Mr. Davis. Shall we talk about sedition?"

His wife moves about in the room above, comforting the child. He hears her footsteps, her soft voice, the child's subsiding cries. Sometimes he fears they are spoiling the child; it meant so very much to them—between them—was so hard to conceive. And he fears the fault was his, borne on the failure of his first marriage.

He hears the mobile start up as the baby is put back into her bed, and as the music winds down, he sits quietly thinking. He was seven. His mother went away and brought back the new child. . . .

(The child was sleeping: this was the whole house.

He lay in bed, watching the motion of carlights on the ceiling, until his parents were in bed. Then, quietly, he crept down the hall into the nursery and stood before the cot, looking down at the fragile, strange little body, infuriated at its helplessness. He raised one hand and hit it, hit it again, again—until the baby's screams woke his mother and she came running across the house.

By the time she got there he had the child in his arms and was cradling it and crooning and crying softly.)

When his wife came back down into the living room, he was thinking of small bodies, dark like Indians. They were lying strangely on fields, their arms and legs at odd angles.

"She was just frightened," his wife told him.

"Jane," he said, "I can't do it. Not any longer. No more."

"Your calls, your . . . arrangements . . . were naturally relayed to us, you see. You understand: patriotism, duty. A going thing these days."

He looked down at the paper under Davis' arm.

"You're a practical man, Mr. Davis. You understand how things work, how things get done, otherwise you wouldn't be where you are now." The smile again, the tightening skin. "And you're an important man, a very important man." He came up straight in the chair, leaned forward. "But you know that, don't you? That's why you're here tonight, why you made those . . . arrangements . . . this afternoon. It works both ways. But the thing you have to ask yourself is: *how* important?"

He leaned farther forward, putting out one hand to the silver frame. He turned it around and looked at it closely for several moments. "Your wife." Then put it back on the desk, facing Davis. "A beautiful woman." When he put his hand up to his lips, Davis noticed that the cigarette, with its glowing conical end, looked like a bullet.

"Let's see, how old *is* your son now—Dave, isn't it? Nineteen? History at Yale, if I remember right. . . ."

Davis nodded.

"You're quite fortunate that he hasn't got himself involved with the Secessionists, you know: it's a cancer that claims more and more of our best young minds. The government's tolerated them up till now, but we've begun picking up some of the ringleaders, you see. . . ." He punched his cigarette into the ashes, pushing it forward as though he were closing a switch. "Domestic strife. That's bad for a country. Splits it up, makes it dissipate its efforts—like a neurotic—makes it look bad. Besides, we need the troops. First the Black Riots, the coalition monopolies; then the Student Alliance, and now the Student Secession. A silly protest—symbolic at best—but it demands attention the government could put to better use elsewhere."

He forked another cigarette out from under his coat, lit it, breathed smoke.

"I'm sure you'll understand that."

There were several moments of silence, in which Davis sat looking at the photograph the man had replaced square on the blotter. Light from the lamp glared on the glass, obscuring the faces of his wife and son, the shape of their house behind. Smoke rose, heaving softly, into the light.

"You might be interested to know there's a rumor going around to the effect that the Secession is being indirectly funded by your company. An outright lie of course. But

I've heard that some of the student leaders are prepared
to testify to it—one wonders what their motives might be.
And——"

"Headlights, Carl," the man at the door interrupted.

"Watch them." Without moving his head. "And I'm
afraid . . . well, let's just say certain people—and groups
—they might be a little upset with you. If the story got
out?"

"Gone. The watchman."

"Time?"

"Twelve."

"On schedule."

The yardlights went off as the watchman's car passed
through the west gate. Lee would be sitting in the booth
now, radio on against regulations, eating the sandwiches
his wife packed up in polyethylene. Davis looked out the
window, blinking.

There were clouds the color of ashes.

Evening climbs the towers, tanks, derricks. From the
window he can see only the plant and a slab of gray sky
that seems to him now pendulous, impending. He knows
that the tiny shapes moving among the scaffolding far
away across the concrete, and against that sky, are men.

Father—

A product (as you say) essen-
tial to the security of the nation. . . .

"The chemical reaction melts the flesh,
and the flesh runs down their faces onto
their chests and it sits there and it grows
there. These children can't turn their heads,
they are so thick with flesh. And when gan-

grene sets in, they cut off their hands, their
fingers, or feet." "Their eyes are gone,
melted away, and their ears are lumps of
raw flesh, fused shut; they resemble nothing
so much as huge pink cauliflowers, rotting."
"Twenty civilians for every soldier."—Some
relics of our past.

Ad hominem! Yes, I know how quick
you'll be to think that—but does it matter?
The fact remains: we are commiting a
crime—a sin, to use a word that you pos-
sess—of silence. That at least, at the very
least. And what can it matter, *how* you find
the darkness, *how* you finally penetrate to
the horrible canyons behind all the words?

One has to decide: how much does he
owe to his society—how much can that society demand of him—and how much can
he, must he, keep to himself. Which of the
million strings, the cat's-cradles binding
him to all the other people, seem to him
most important? It's for every man, that
single question. And I, *for* myself, have
finally found the answer, finally know. . . .

Which is, in turn, my answer to your
letter. The letter you dictated to Betty.

Love,
David

Gradually it grows dark outside, sinking from steel-gray
to plum to black, and finally he is staring at a vague
reflection of himself and the office in the glare of the
overhead light.

He withdraws and crosses the room to shut off the
light; sits at his desk and touches the intercom.

"Betty, before you leave, could you get my wife on the phone?"

"Yes sir."

"And then Jim Morrison at United Press."

"Yes sir."

Waiting, he turns on the desk lamp and sits in a small circle of light.

"Now, you take Santos at Allied, there's a good man— and I understand he's just been given a grant to expand operations. A small plant, but quite efficient. Something about a new thickening agent, better than polystyrene, some say. Worked his way up from a technician. Now he's got a fine home, a beautiful wife, three sons—all of them draft age, as it happens. About the same age as Dave, as a matter of fact." He smiled again. "Always someone next in line, right Mr. Davis?"

The man lit another cigarette and sat in the chair, smoking, watching. His arm went up to his mouth, away from his mouth. Up, down. It reminded Davis of blinking neons. He looked down at the papers under his arm; he'd spent hours on them and now it was as though he saw them for the first time, as though someone had forged his writing and left them here on the desk. They seemed so distant, so unreal. . . .

The thin man was smiling at him. "Is it strong enough, Mr. Davis? Is it after all what you wanted so badly to say?" He reached out and took the papers from under Davis' arms. Smiling, and squinting in the dim light, he read them. His cigarette burned down in the ashtray.

Finally, he looked up.

"Quite good, actually. That part about the babies—

you'd have made a good journalist. Ad hominem, of course." He stubbed out the cigarette. "But what's a logical fallacy or two when you're on the side of The Good. . . ." He looked back down at the papers. "You know, I never noticed before, but the word has an Oriental ring to it."

The man at the door put his hand on the knob: "Twelve-twenty, Carl."

"Then that's about all, Mr. Davis. I hope you'll remember our little talk tonight, should you get the urge again to . . . express yourself?" He put a hand on the desk and stood. The hand moved. Ashes spilled out onto the red carpet. "Oh, I *am* sorry, Mr. Davis." He rolled the statement up, stuffed it into his coat pocket. "We'll be in touch. It's been nice talking with you."

The other was already in the hall. The thin one walked slowly across the room and turned back for a moment at the door.

"The papers wouldn't have printed it anyway, you know: their duty. Patriotism. It's a going thing, these days."

And then they were gone, the door closed.

Davis sat listening to their footsteps fade away, loud and hollow in the hall. Then the clank and whirr of an elevator descending. Then silence. He noticed how the top sheet of the pad was covered with pressure marks.

(*For God's sake, Dave, don't give up. Don't let go.*)

He got up and walked to the window. He looked out on the towers, tanks, derricks erecting themselves against the sky; at the clouds that moved among them. His breath made circles of frost on the glass. He smelled the spilt ashes.

The two men came out of the building below him—

walking slowly, talking, finished with their night's work
—and got into their car. Seconds apart, the domelight
went on-off, on-off, with the two doors; then there was
only the thin one's cigarette moving in the darkness: up.
And down.

Finally the headlights came on and lay out along the
field of concrete like two Doric columns. Dimly, Davis
could hear the engine. And now he spoke softly to the
room that watched over his shoulder, something remembered from college, and now the circle of frost spread, the
circle of frost deepened and tugged at the light. . . .

"But that was his duty, he only did his duty—"
Said Judy, said the Judy, said poor Judy to the string.

Davis stood staring at his own breath, at his face in the
circle of frost. The edge darkened and began to recede;
circle by circle, it crept ever inward, vanishing finally into
its own center.

When the pane cleared, the car was gone. And then the
dark was absolute.

The darkness that surrounds us.

London
March 1968

Front & Centaur

So they went to London and they got a flat together on Portobello Road and they wrote.

Down in the street dogs shoved their snouts into tincans, scraping them along the pavement; babies waited for mothers outside the shops in prams; the pubs burned brilliantly. One of them had observed: "My urine steams in British bathrooms!" Also, they had discovered that plugs of linoleum would appease the electricity meter.

Dave Dunder was the tall one, the thin one with a voice like vanilla pudding, and he wrote westerns. Bill Blitzen was short, with legs like two huge bolognas, eyes that jumped on you if you came too close, and a burning red bush of a beard; he turned out true confessions, four a week, and ghostwrote poetry (by a machine he had invented) on the side. Seeing them at opposite ends of a bench in Regents Park, a man would automatically tilt his head to one side, trying to get the world back to a level. When they walked together, Dunder leaned out over Blitzen from behind, sheltering him from sun and rain. They wore two halves of a six-foot muffler, ripped in two by Dunder one evening in "a moment of excessive charity." And they were in love with the same girl.

Tonight, after their customary mutual reading from the *Ulysses* nighttown sequence, they had boiled up the day's left-over coffee and gone to work at their desks, which faced one another across the length of the room. A stein of soupy coffee steamed on each desk. With the flat they had inherited an electric heater. It had two filaments, one of which Blitzen had removed, extending it on wires across the room and hanging it from the ceiling directly before his face.

It was in the general order of things that Blitzen would sit down, ringed by sweets and smoking apparatus and small jugs of beer, and set immediately to work. For the next several hours, until he was through for the night, his typewriter would cluck away furiously, steadily, one hand now and again snaking out to light a cigarette on the heater—while Dunder would be ripping sheets off his pad, balling them up and throwing them toward the corner; jerkily spurting and halting toward the end of a story; rewriting, trying to find some pattern in it all, revising and banging away angrily at his desktop.

So Dave had fallen to work tonight, laboring, like a man constipated for weeks, at the final revision of a short-short, and was soon lost to the ordered confusion of pages, inserts, scribbling and deletion. An hour later, suddenly noticing the silence at the other end of the room, he looked up. There was a walrus sitting in Bill's chair, smoking a meerschaum pipe.

"I say," he said. "You're looking rather odd tonight, Blitzen."

The walrus glanced up, then looked back down at his work. "You should talk," it said. "That's the silliest red nose I've ever seen—and I've seen a few in my time." Then, almost as an afterthought: "Now is the time, you know." At these words, Dave's desk became a hippopotamus and went galloping off toward the bathroom. The floor creaked threateningly.

Dave sat for a moment staring at the little circles on the linoleum where the desklegs had been. As he watched, they suddenly started moving and scuttled off into a dark corner. He uncrossed his leg and his hoof clattered on the floor.

"Now that *is* strange," he said. "Blitzen, do you think you could take a minute off? I really think we should talk this over." Having finished its pipe, the walrus was methodically going through all the drawers, eating every scrap of paper it could find. There was a small but growing pile of paperclips on the desk before it.

"Now is the time," the walrus said again. It bent its head and its tusk scraped along the desk, scattering paperclips: one pinged into the wastebasket. Minnesota was never like this.

"Yes, it would appear to be, wouldn't it?"

The papers were turning into doves, which flapped away from the walrus and out the window. Dunder ducked to avoid one and caught a glimpse of print on its wing as it went wheeling frantically past him. A moment later it came back to the window with an olive leaf in its beak.

"But I really think we should put our heads together and give this a bit of thought. What are we going to eat, for example? I'll wager there's not a bale of hay in the house. . . . Is that right: hay?" As he said this, the rug began to grow. "And what will Berenice say if she comes and finds us like this?" The rug was now three feet tall, a thick field of grass. Not far away, Dunder could make out his beaded belt lying like a snake across the top of the greenery, sunning itself. The rug rustled with the movement of many small things scurrying to safety. He jumped to his feet just as his own chair went hopping off into it; for several seconds he could see its back, bobbing up and down—then the grass was too high.

Dunder stood poking gently at the grass with his antlers, trying to decide what to do. What was needed was organization, some careful thought, a system. They could cope.

And with a *pop*, flowers began growing off the wallpaper, small bunches of orchids, slowly drooping towards the floor under the weight of their heads as the stems lengthened like spaghetti. Feathers from the pillows had gathered in cloudy masses high in the room, and when they parted for a moment, Dunder saw things like waterbugs skimming across the surface of the blue ceiling.

He heard a snuffling at the base of the kitchen door; a rather foreboding growl issued from the bedroom. And then the walrus came crashing through the grass and yellow blossoms, muttering to itself: "Berenice . . . I don't know what we saw in her in the first place. She's awfully *thin*, you know." It looked up, saw Dunder standing there, and went running, terrified, back into the growth. After a bit, Dunder could hear it far away, gam-

boling in bucolic splendor. Then there was a mighty
splash—

And a knock at the door. It was getting dark; Dunder's
nose began to glow like an electric cherry.

And another knock.

And another knock.

And another knock.

"Go away," a voice gurgled from across the room.

A key rattled in the lock and the door opened. Berenice
stood there naked, clothes and the makings for a late tea
under her arm. Her hair was done up in a honeycomb and
a silver disk hung against her chest, like the moon sighted
between two hills.

"Cut it out, fellows," she said.

"Glug. Glug."

"Now is the time," Dunder told her. That was all he
could think to say. Minnesota had certainly never been
like this.

"What does this *mean?*" she asked, coming a few steps
into the room. "Are you trying to get rid of me? Don't you
think you owe me an explanation at least? You don't want
me to come around to see you anymore."

"Oh, no," Dunder said. "It's just——"

"That's what always happens. They always do this, it
always turns out like this in the end."

"Go away," the walrus bellowed from deep in the
weeds.

"See? See? God knows I try to make them love me; it's
not my fault. I do everything I can——"

"Now is the time." Dunder. He was rapidly running out
of words.

"——and in the end it's always like this, this always
happens."

Far away, they could hear the walrus dancing a softshoe and singing *America the Beautiful.*

"I'm pregnant, you know. . . . We used to be so happy. Damn you. Want accretion, the James-Lange theory of emotion. I thought you would *amount* to something. What happened to us? Epithesis, existentialism. I love you."

It was beginning to rain. "It's raining, deer," she said, then giggled horribly. They huddled together in the fireplace, warm and talking quietly, watching the rain come down outside. "What will become of little William David now? That's what I decided to call him, see." Together they nibbled at chocolate biscuits. She fed him, offering each biscuit on her open hand after taking a few bites, and he chewed them daintily. He ran his tongue along the soft skin at the base of her thumb. She thought it was the walrus' dance which had brought on the rain. "Or do you think David William sounds better?"

There was a polite cough at the door: Dunder and Berenice turned together. A handsome young unicorn stood outside in a shaft of sunlight, tossing its head so that the mane swirled down around its horn.

"Come live with me and be my love," it said.

Dunder was aware of the walrus standing behind him, peering furtively out from the bushes. "Minnesota was never like this," it whispered.

Berenice stood and with one last look at Dunder, a look full of scorn and contempt, walked to the unicorn and leapt onto its great ridged back. "*Americans!*" she said.

The unicorn nodded and swung its tail to brush away a fly that had settled on her bare bottom, in the dimple at the top of her left buttock. They turned and rode off together down the hall toward Cheshire. . . .

And nothing's been the same since.

Enclave

A bright yellow room. The room is empty save for a table
and two chairs, a bed, a small animal cage beside it,
books. The bed is steel-framed, the headboard and base
composed of slender steel rods; it creaks with every movement in the room, whether or not the bed is itself occupied. The cage is of the same steel rods, but painted a
chrome-bright green (those of the bed are white), and is
approximately 2 by 3 feet. It appears to be empty; but
harsh, metallic sounds (gratings, clicks) issue from within
it throughout the play. The cage is supported, at the level
of the bed, atop a stack of oversize books like those which
contain reproductions of paintings, or like "coffee-table"
books. The stage is in fact literally overwhelmed by the
presence and the *fact* of books; filled with them; they are
piled on the floor, the bed, against the walls. They are of

every possible size, yet each is either scarlet or sky-blue. Some are neatly, squarely stacked; others are leaning in disorder against the walls and bed; some are in precisely swirled columns, like spiral staircases, and reach as high as 8 to 10 feet. In one corner there is a pile of them, hundreds of books, paperbacks, magazines, dumped there at random and looking as though the entire mass would collapse were one to touch it, even come too close.

A woman is standing at the blank, yellow wall stage-right, dressed in formal eveningwear, staring *out*, as though a window existed there. A man is on the bed. He is naked, books piled under and around him. (Because of the books we cannot actually see that he is naked.) After several moments, during which the tableau is held, the man speaks. Even then, there is no movement.

—Well?

The woman continues to stare *out*. Finally he speaks again.

—What colour uniforms?

She parts her lips. Begins slowly, quietly.

—Pink. . . ? No. No, they're naked. They're naked this time.

—Students.

—No. . . . No, they look too young.

—Soldiers then.

—Some of them have painted the top of their bodies brown. . . .

—Or veterans.

—Some of the children are wearing armbands. . . .

—The old woman, is she still out there?

—She's making a speech. She has to stop every few seconds to put her teeth back in. They keep falling out.

Pause. The woman continues to stare fixedly at the wall. The man picks up a book, thumbs through it, tosses it back onto the bed.

—The bombs?

—Of course. You can't hear them? They haven't stopped for weeks now. Not for a moment, a second.

The man shrugs. Books shift on the bed, slide down his body.

—You get used to them I suppose. Don't notice. After a while.

—Do you think it's really America?

—Don't be silly. Who else would it be.

As he speaks these lines the man is pushing books away from him, struggling out of the bed. Several books fall on to the floor—the greatest quantity at the exact moment his *feet* touch the floor. Simultaneously the rest, those remaining on the bed, collapse together into a compost heap. The man rises and walks distractedly among the stacks of books, vaguely towards the tea table. (He contrives to remain partially under cover of the books, so that we never in fact see that he is naked at any time during the play.) The woman is still standing at the wall, motionless, "looking out."

—There's a priest. . . .

The man begins to make tea. Sounds: the metallic clicks and grating from the animal cage (almost metronomic), the creaking of the bed at every movement he makes, the whistle of the teakettle. Absolute silence "outside."

—He's walking among the bodies. He has a ring on each hand. One has a question mark on it, the other has an x. Sharp edges, like razors. He's branding the wounded and dead. Whenever anyone argues with him he immediately pushes the x into their forehead. Or their cheeks.

The man is pouring tea at the table. The table and chairs, the cups are steel, the same colour as the cage.

—The farmers are standing around the rice paddies. They're throwing firecrackers when the others come too close. . . .

—Ready dear.

—There's a sniper on top of the Eiffel Tower. . . .

—Come dear.

—Indians are coming down the canals in canoes. They have crossbows. And beards. And steel helmets with horns on them. . . .

The woman turns suddenly, goes to the table, sits. *Long pause.* The man and the woman drink their tea. *Long pause.* The sounds from cage and bed continue; also, the teakettle is still whistling. (It continues to whistle for the duration of the play.) Spoons clink, mouths slurp, the woman speaks.

—Where are the children dear? have you seen them lately? There are ten . . . no, eleven . . . of them.

—What? I think they went out. To play. Are there really that many now?

—What? I think so. Yes, at least eleven. When did they leave?

—What? I don't know. A few days ago I think.

Pause.

—*You* haven't been going out. To work I mean.

The woman pauses, stares across the table at the man.

—What was it you used to do?

—I was a physicist.

—But what did you *do?*

Long pause. The man frowns in concentration; then smiles.

—Oh, you know. Entropy, information theory, stuff like that . . . I think.

The woman sips tea, stares into the cup.

—We're out of tea again.

—Mmmm. They dumped it all in the harbor.

—Sassafras.

—Mmmm. It's growing in the closet.

—Which one?

—Well, all of them as a matter of fact.

—The roach spray didn't work.

(He stares into his teacup.)

There is a crash, as of glass shattering, and a heavy object strikes the floor. The man leaps to his feet. The woman drops her cup, speaks.

—Mind the glass. It shattered the window, you might get a nasty cut.

—I'm not going near it. It might be a bomb.

—Don't be silly, it's a brick. Not a bomb. And there's a message wrapped around it.

—It could still be a bomb.

—But it's not even ticking or anything, it's perfectly quiet.

—So much the worse. *I* regard that as highly suspicious.

—It's a brick.

—But it has words on it. You have to admit it has words on it.

—Of course. A message would have words, wouldn't it.

The man pauses, considering:

—Not necessarily. . . . What language?

—English.

—*See!* I told you. I'm-not-going-near-it.

They sit to their tea again. The brick remains on the floor, its message and presence ignored. The teakettle continues to whistle; the cage to give forth its clicks and rasps; the bed to creak at every movement the man makes. The woman begins to read from a newspaper. The man glances at the wall from time to time, nervously. They carry on with their afternoon tea. Finally the woman speaks, without looking up from the paper.

—Why don't you go look out dear. You look upset, that would help you.

—No. No I was . . . just . . . wondering.

There is a long pause; to the other sounds is added, now, the rustling of paper. After a while the woman says, idly,

—Someone just applied to Lloyd's to insure the human race.

—Incredible!

—Hmmm.

—They're still putting out the papers.

—Hmmm.

—We don't even subscribe to one you know.

—What?

—Where did you get it?

—What.

—The paper, where did you get it?

—O. It was on the floor, by the front door. Someone had shoved it under the door, I suppose.

—When?

Pause.

—I don't know. I just noticed it today, this morning, it could have been there longer.

The woman pages through the paper:

—There's no date on it, anywhere.

—Of course not. There wouldn't be, would there. How would they know.

The man suddenly gets up and walks to the wall. As he "looks out," the sounds stop. The bed (which went into a frenzy when he stood); the teakettle. *Then* the sounds from the cage—he notices and turns very quickly. Walks toward the cage. Stands staring down at it.

—It died. You flushed it down the lav. Last week. Or the week before. . . .

The man stares at the woman for several seconds, then goes back to the wall. Motionless there, he assumes the position the woman held at the play's beginning. Now we can hear the sounds outside. Bombs, shouts, guns.

A single scream.

Slice of Universe

The guidebirds beat their tiny wings and moaned to one another across the ceiling of the flightroom. (Fright, complaint, confusion, fear: *Where was home, where was home?* So far, so far.) Half sunk in the suckweed, Merler floated under the blister-cages. The birds' cries crept and rolled on tandem oscilloscopes: the ship took up those lines, tossed them out to the void, moved along them.

Loved Merler, I come to report—and Whorlin stofted into the room, trailing suckweed, upper of his twin external tongues clucking in the "Most important" quadrant. Unnecessary, since he was using one tongue—but Whorlin was a stylist, with a reputation to consider.

Merler inhaled, bloated, came up partway out of the suckweed. Then bestupt his tongue in a perfectly chosen reply: *I wish your words to my heart.*

For a moment Whorlin paused. He envied such a natural, easy style. His own tended toward artifice, abstraction: too careful, too considered. He couldn't match Merler's vitality, and that vitality seemed almost effortless.

(*Poor, o poor birdies. Took our homes away. O poor poor birds.* And fluttered their useless wings.)

Whorlin vurked *I have just found* and the stylistic device *Borgman furfth at leisure* in harmony on his external tongues, threading it throughout with a rhythm-of-discovery clicked in paradiddle on his internal tongues, finally adding the odor complex that signified *I seed my words in your heart and pray for their growth.*

Merler tipped sideways on the sand. *Schlupp!* his roots shot up into their sheaths. He rolled back upward and came off the pool. Wetness flowed down him, staining the sand.

Whorlin accepted respect; slipped his tongue into out-phase and began to fugue on discoveries. Almost casually, Merler broke in with a haunting, improvised counterpoint on the theme *My heart is fast, things are slow,* simultaneously chiming his nether tongue several octaves higher and in discord on *Words words words, they breathe and breed.*

Whorlin furled a root out toward the wetness and kurthed his apology in one of the more difficult standard études. Merler, complying, beat out the motif *My heart waits. . . .*

Whorlin listened for a moment, then complimented Merler on his attacks.

Yes, regard, obligation. Inner tongues, obligatto: *My words can never approach your fineness.* Throat-tongue, motif repeated, beating: *My heart waits. . . .*

(*Home, home, where is home? Where are they taking*

us poor, poor birds? Where are they taking the birdies' ship? Hurt. Hurt the poor poor birds.)

With some regret, Whorlin clicked the rhythm-of-directness on his internal tongues, overtoning that they must sometime ensemble together.

A man on Earth, he vurked, and caught a rhythm-of-wonder from Merler. He developed a theme for Earth; halfway through, Merler harmonized acceptance. Then: *My heart waits,* throbbing.

I have just borged.

Acceptance.

A man.

Rhythm-of-wonder.

Whorlin introduced the motif for science, then overtured discovery, improvising on it until Merler rhymed him.

The universe is finite, he went on, developing this theme, concluding with an obligatto *Most important* on his upper external tongue.

Merler motifed the rhythm-of-wonder. Each time his tongues found a beat, Whorlin could feel the seeping life within him; his roots fell away from the wetness, crept back over the sand toward their sheath. Merler paused, then rhythmed completeness.

The work is correct, Whorlin responded. *I have borged the symbols closely.* He buzzed his throat-tongue and added a sketchy odor complex, transferring respect back to Merler.

(*Home, home. Birdies will die away from home. So far, so far. Dead ship, away from home. Where is home? Pity us poor poor birds.*)

This means we shall run out of worlds, Merler vurked.

It borges so.

We shall have no new worlds to find. Image and accompaniment began to rise behind his words.

Acceptance, limitation. *So far ahead it has no meaning. Far, far ahead. Even for us, the two of us.*

Rhythm-of-wonder, swelling. *We shall have no new worlds, new wonders, new voices. We, whose only work and purpose is discovery, whose only love is the voyage. We who have made empty space our friend these million years. . . .*

So far ahead we have no symbols for it.

Rhythm-of-wonder. The phase of sadness. *It is enough to know someday there will be no more.* The words dropped onto his tongues and lay there, gathering things —emotion, image, resonance—about them, and then, just before it seemed they must die, escaping. His eyes drooped. His roots lay limply out on the sand.

Whorlin beat out completeness in unity against his palates. And then he listened as Merler built a poem of loss about them in the room of pools and weed and sand: a warm hollow thing, filled with sadness and covered over with wonder and love: a small thing, strange with fur, that broke the heart. And for the first time Whorlin understood the beauty and power of Merler's vurking, the limits of his own trained precision. As Merler's tongues clicked and fluttered and sang. . . .

He told of a people which had come from the sea onto the orange plains and rolling, wine hills of a huge double-sunned world; had come and carved the land to their likeness. Then when the land was filled and familiar they had felt again the drag of that sea against their chest and had, some of them, returned. And when even the sea was known, when there were no new things, the people had looked above them and found new worlds, had sailed out to larger seas, seas they believed would never end. They had stepstoned on stars to step among these worlds: quietly, reverently, always listening for new musics, new life. And this in turn became *their* life, the way and beauty of their lives: to be always searching for new things, to be close to beginnings, eavesdroppers to the wonders of a universe. With their birds they had tied world to world, sun to sun, had begun to fill space itself with the paths of their traveling. They were a long-lived people, and one man could in his time be a part of many worlds. . . .

And he spoke of things that end. Of the birds. Their ship. The two of them, Merler and Whorlin, away from home a thousand years. And someday the birds would die, the ship be useless, the two of them marooned, alone. Alone—and all the worlds waiting. But not enough: someday there would be no more. Even worlds had their end. . . .

His words resounded in the room. Image dropped away and only the sounds were left; then those too were gone, lost in the sand and the weed-crammed pools. The room was quiet with the breathing murmur of controls. Odors drifted, fading, in the air.

It is sadness, Whorlin vurked after a while. Then, respectfully, he reversed his head and departed the flight-room, leaving a patch of wetness behind on the sand.

Merler stood looking after him for a moment, then rolled back onto the suckweed and sent his roots deep down into the living fluid below. He exhaled and his body collapsed around him, sank into the weed. He looked at his bank of controls, at the two dark spots of dampness out on the sand. He spun his eyes in concentration. The guidebirds whined.

(Poor, o poor birdies. Took our homes away. So far, so far. O poor poor birds.)

And outside, the darkness that somewhere, someday had an end—this darkness touched softly at the front of their ship, stroked along it, and fell off into the vacuum behind.

III

The Anxiety in the Eyes
of the Cricket

Afterwards, they sat together on the terrace patio smoking.

Behind them on the steel slab, the house, with its forty rooms separate as the chambers of a nautilus, stood like something grown up out of the hill. The steel extended several yards down into the gray ash-like soil, steel scaffolding still farther, to the baserock. Behind the house, for more than a mile, the ground was pitted into a bare colorless canyon, scooped out and pushed forward to form this hill.

Jerry had just come from the East, with his arm torn loose from the socket and one eye half-closed on itself. Passage was difficult these days. He had come on impulse;

felt the pull one morning and responded to it as he had so many times before. In China now, and certain portions of India, at least one small part of the economy would be finding itself empty and crippled.

"How is it there now?" his friend had asked as he smoothed on the salves, wheeled the square white machines, tables, glass chambers across the floor in the bare white room, pulling Jerry's body, wrecked by disease, malnutrition and damage, back into a single organism. For Jerry, accustomed to the tonal languages of the East and its strange inverted thinking, the rough, assonant rhythms of his friend's speech, its somehow Parnassian starkness, were oddly disturbing: a disorientation which was to continue, in fact to grow ever more persistent. English, which had become the French of the last century, then a kind of mirror-image Mandarin—sparse and subtle in its rhythms but yielding great resonance, a quality first noted by midcentury mystery writers and exploited by certain American poets—was now atrophying, dying in upon itself. Words tumbled readily off the tongue, too readily, in brief economical strings like a kind of verbal semaphore, and increasingly had relevance only to themselves—poets, Jerry knew from personal experience, were having a hard time of it. Simultaneously, the tone-rich Chinese language was bursting open, becoming rich and resonant in substance as well, coming more to resemble the evocative, implicit poetry of its written form, now in turn increasingly linear and stylised. What was the precise relationship of language to society, of spoken to written language? English, with its truncated bursts of energy; the flow of Mandarin. Did entropy in one predict, or establish, entropy in the other? Which way did the influence flow? Jerry wondered.

"Better," he had answered his friend.

"You have a perverse love for ambiguity, Jerry. Better than before, or better than here?" He selected a scalpel from the tray and moved behind Jerry with it. The shoulder was anaesthetised, but Jerry could feel the warm blood running down his ribs.

In answer, he had simply grinned.

Now two Drambuies sat on the red enamel deck-table between them and the taste of the thick, sweet liqueur was still in Jerry's mouth. Another glass, a tumbler, was partly filled with cigarettes of strong black tobacco—perique, Jerry thought, from the smell—wrapped in meerschaum papers. His friend held one of these, hand cupped against his ear and elbow on the chair arm, violet smoke pouring out around his bleached white hair. He was dressed in black silk pajamas, and Jerry wore a similar pair; his own Western clothes had been spattered and torn when he arrived. Near the centre of the table, almost touching the pole which suspended a Union Jack umbrella out over them, sat a wineglass left out overnight. It was half full. A delicate crust of ice skimmed the deep red surface and, thinner still, ran up the side of the glass along which, yesterday afternoon, Jerry had sipped the wine. Its gold stem was as thin as a flower stalk, the glass itself as large as a man's cupped hands, the base formed of three long, twisted gold tendrils, like roots or the foot of a bird. Jerry, newly aware of color, sat staring for some time at the form all this took, then reached out and shifted the glasses. His right arm and shoulder, the damaged ones, were in the sun, and ached slightly. No use—just another form. The umbrella's gold-braid fringe was still. There was no wind, no movement.

Far below, a small private boat slid through the black

water, lugging a makeshift barge—actually more a raft—
behind it on a single thick cable. There were still those
who cared. The barge was filled with the bodies of the
suicides, stacked randomly crisscross on the flat deck like
matches in an ashtray. Miles away down the river, where
the boat was headed, the flames showed dim in the sun.
Jerry imagined for a moment that he could hear the
popping of flame within flame as it reached out and ran
across the bodies, choosing eyeballs which would explode
into gray sizzling mush, lips which would burst and let out
fresh pink meat, soft swollen testicles. The chaos, he
knew, was apparent. An illusion. The real problem was
over-organisation, entropy, the seeming confusion only the
final struggle against its imposition. Fact and metaphysics
were, finally, the same thing.

Looking back to the barge he thought of Gericault, and
only then noticed the words stenciled in bright red letters
across the boat's prow: *The Medusa*. Irony or humor? He
wondered. Was it form or quality that separated them—
if, indeed, the distinction could exist anymore, if any
could. A defense, he supposed, but what sort of man——

"It's a question of guilt." Michael snapped the cigarette
away from him and it tumbled through its own smoke out
into space, down along the cliff and into the water, to
collect with the refuse and bodies which floated several
feet out from each bank.

Jerry shrugged. "For some." A knife stabbed into the
socket of his shoulder and twisted, then quickly with-
drew, leaving behind a dull throb. He lifted his Drambuie
and looked across the rim to the city far below beyond the
water. The city was completely still; nothing moved inside it. "You?"

"Perhaps. . . ."

"You told them the city would kill them. You predicted that much." Jerry found it difficult to look at his friend. Difficult, too, to speak in the old language: he had no right here, he didn't belong. Not any longer. He was intruding.

"I predicted everything. Save for the end. . . ."

"They struck first."

"And the city is dying. Like the rest." He took another cigarette from the tumbler. The remaining ones toppled, like jackstraws, into a new pattern. "But do they know? If they knew . . ." His hand stopped in mid-wave and fell back onto the chair—too much effort. And no reward. It didn't matter. It was too late.

He struck a match and for a moment Jerry shrank back in his chair, then overcame the reflex. But when Michael pushed the tumbler toward him, he shook his head violently.

Jerry said, "They might do something?"

His friend sat smoking, staring out across the water. Finally he spoke, only his lips moving.

"The boats. From the States. They are coming in at the rate of ten, twelve a day now. The holds are full, the decks as well. The bodies are stiff as boards. They say the crews have learned to walk across them without noticing they're there. Or what they are. As though they *were* boards. Southampton is packed with them, miles out to sea, the Pool of London filled months ago."

"And you began it? By telling them——"

"Jerry. That was after I came here, after all this was built. You should understand. You've been here a week now." (That morning as they lay side by side in bed, exhausted, Michael had said, "Jerry, you are the most religious person I know. I'm in awe of that, it frightens me.")

"And tomorrow I leave."

Michael looked up at the sky. It was choked with smoke from the burning bodies, smoke that hung motionless in dense, shapeless clouds, like clots of blood. "Where will you go?"

Jerry paused. "Into the city. I'd like to borrow your boat." Suddenly he caught the smell of cabbage from the gardens beside the house. There were a dozen varieties— it was one of the few things which would grow from the soil now—and the smells of each mingled together, though Jerry felt, if he wanted, he could separate every one, like picking out individual strands of seaweed. A small plot of artificial flowers stood beside the cabbage, their bright red and yellow heads lost to the sheer mass of greenery. "I have a family there."

Michael said nothing for several moments, then looked down at the river, away from the smoke. The boat was almost out of sight; only the barge showed. "You never mentioned that before. You knew——"

"That it would be against your principles? Yes, but I care more for you than for your principles. I haven't seen them for years. But now. . . ."

"You're amused, Jerry? That I hold to my own morality, even in all this?" He sipped at his Drambuie, then suddenly threw the glass away from him out over the cliff. The liquid spilled, spinning in a flat disc and, while the glass plunged downward, seeming to hesitate before it followed, breaking into a loose shower. "No. Of course you're not. I had the boat destroyed. Burned. I'm sorry."

"I'll find a way."

Michael looked at Jerry, opened his mouth, then shut it again and turned away.

"A wife," Jerry said. "And a son." It might be reassuring, it might help him, if his friend wept. The separation, whatever, would not be an easy one.

Michael nodded quietly. He reached up to the monogrammed pocket and took out a boiled egg, already peeled, put it on his palm then returned to the pocket and brought out a small silver spoon between his first two fingers. The spoon dangled loosely between them; the hands were pale, bloated white, the fingers perfectly straight, joints hardly creased at all. He knew from experience that offering one to Jerry would be a futile gesture. But a gesture these days, however futile. . . . He looked across the table at his friend and Jerry shook his head. His hair was short now, shorter than Michael had ever seen it. He had arrived with hair filthy and tangled; repairing him, grooming him, Michael had no choice but to cut it. He remembered how Jerry had sat staring into the mirror, very still, watching the fine, tangled black strands fall onto his shoulders and tumble down across his chest and arms as his friend moved behind him, manipulating the scissors.

Michael lived on eggs (difficult as they were to obtain) and Drambuie, but had been unable to discover what kept Jerry going. He had never seen him eat. Anything. It seemed to him that Jerry grew thinner every day, and there had been, these past few days, a weakness in his movements—a weakness Michael had first noticed in bed, and one all the more remarkable for its contrast to Jerry's strong, deep voice. What strength he had left seemed to have gathered in that voice, and in his hands, and even here there was a quality of stillness.

Michael lifted the egg in his palm and looked at it against the smoke-swaddled air. So simple, symmetrical. Egg and hand were barely distinguishable. His friend's voice came across the table to him, soft now, and low.

"It's not the effect, but the *fact,* that one finds intolerable."

Michael made no response. Neither of them moved, looking out across the water toward the city.

"They are there. Inexorable, ineffable, intolerable."

"If such things as facts exist . . . ?"

"The absence of fact, in effects, *becomes* fact."

"Yes. I suppose. . . ." What had he begun to say? It was lost, whatever. He shook his head and looked back at the egg. "Don't try to help me, Jerry." He stabbed the spoon into the egg and a plug of white flew off into the air, landing just past the patio and throwing up a fine cloud of ashy dust. Jerry watched as he scooped out a daub of dull yellow on the tip of the tiny spade the size of a fingernail and lifted it to his mouth. A pink tongue met it, rolled back into the mouth. Jerry wondered idly how the egg would taste on top of Drambuie. He lifted his own glass, empty now, and a drop of the thick liqueur which had gathered back to the bottom slid slowly down it to his tongue. The egg was smashed into dry fragments now on his friend's open hand.

Jerry looked toward the garden. He found himself unable to watch the eating. For the first time he noticed a sign there, a handpainted square on a short stick, almost lost in the rolling folds of cabbage: *Keep ceaseless watch for* COLORADO BEETLES. *They can destroy our potato crops.* He remembered seeing the same sign, years ago, printed then and neatly designed, in every London post office. When he turned back, two more private boats were moving slowly down the water, pulling cluttered barges. A body toppled off one and fell into the wake, drifting, slower still, toward the base of the cliff below.

It was getting dark. Michael had finished the egg and now wiped his palm on his leg, smearing the bits which were left into the dark silk pajamas. He looked down at the barges.

"A question of guilt: is it real? Can it ever be real? Or is it just a word, something conjured up, manufactured, to hide something else we're afraid to face?" He walked to the edge of the patio steel and looked down. (Associations, Jerry thought. I can't stop making associations, not even me. It's the place, I have no right to be here. Mallarmé said that poetry was made from words, not ideas. And Goethe said that whereas an idea was one thing, a word could always be found to replace it. Associations. I can't stop them.) "As you say, a fact. . . . Truth."

Ten feet out from the base of the artificial cliff, the body, propelled by the lazy euphoric wash of boat and barge, collided with the outermost of the bobbing refuse, disrupting it. Finally it came to rest alongside another body, this one gray and bloated from long exposure to the water, and there was only the slight synchronised rippling of movement among the whole. Final remnants of the boats' passage.

"No. A fact."

He turned back to Jerry and smiled. There was a gentle wind from downriver, where the bodies were burning. The umbrella fringe leaned into it, the cabbage swayed all together, its complex leaves rippling lightly backwards, backwards, backwards again. Jerry suddenly remembered something from Wallace Stevens—"All of our ideas come from the natural world: trees = umbrellas."

Was that true. It occurred to him that this was important; he would have to face it. Later. When there was more time.

"To bed now, Jerry?"

"But——"

After a moment he got up and followed his friend, obsessed with the almost imperceptible gray smear on his pajamas. His eyes fastened to it. He thought of his own brown hands: the fingers long and thin, sagging in between the joints, the joints themselves crooked, irregular, the end ones bending back on themselves. Associations. He looked at the cabbage, the sign. He looked back at the smear of egg on Michael's pajamas. He thought of his marriage.

Later that night he woke alone in bed. Michael was standing naked at the window, looking out, with a cigarette in his hand. There was a bright erratic light outside. The radio was on low, Glen Campbell singing, *Gentle on My Mind*. Michael seemed to know instantly that he was awake.

"Jerry. Come to the window."

Jerry slid across the black silk sheets. Were they actually damp or was it simply the absence of a body there, the coldness, which gave that illusion? The floor, at least, was warm. Jerry went across the room and stood beside his friend. Yet when he looked out he felt alone; the sense of Michael as a person faded from him and he knew somehow that it would now be always like this.

The city was burning.

The fires were steady, slow, borne in every building, every house, every street: there was no violence to them, and Jerry, watching, felt a strange sense of peacefulness. Even at this distance, climbing slowly, quietly toward the top of the city, the flames showed on their faces. The black water was full of fire. Only there, in reflection, did the flames become violent.

Without turning from the window Jerry said, "Put that out." Michael stared at him for a moment, then dropped the cigarette and ground it into the carpet with his bare foot.

They stood watching silently. Neither of them moved. It was a single fire now, and as it rose, smoke fluttering upwards, the cloud of black settled down onto the city. They could hear the crackling, explosions, the steady rumble of buildings tumbling back into themselves, pushing the flames higher through the empty corridors.

"They knew," Jerry said finally.

When Michael spoke, his voice was like the click of a revolver rolling onto the next chamber, a beetle shutting its wing case.

"You'll still——"

"Tomorrow," Jerry said. "When the fires have died down."

The fire's light showed on the bodies and refuse against the far bank, making each thing a different object, something apart from the rest. People stood on the bank and looked down into the water. They stood completely still.

"Your wife and son?"

Jerry nodded, and the flames were in his hair. Several minutes passed. Rubble began to fall into the water, pushing the bodies and refuse out away from the bank. They began to drift slowly across the river toward the cliff. Still no one moved. There was no energy left for them. They stood with their heads down, staring into the water, the rubble, refuse, bodies, the reflected flames. Finally, very quietly beside him, Michael broke the silence.

"We'll go together. My boat——"

Jerry cut him off, nodding again, then walked away from him through the doors and onto the patio, where he sat down at the edge of the steel. Michael would know enough not to follow.

He sat there all night, alone, watching the city burn.

Jeremiad

And Jerry left the burning city behind him, returned to the East—to Calcutta, to Burma, Peking, Mashhad. Would he now feel as out of place here as he had in London before he sat on the hill and watched the city burn, the people who stood so still on the harbor and stared into the violent water, the rubble and bodies drifting on the black water toward him?

In Cambodia he was assaulted by a gang of youths, his arm torn loose again in the struggle—and woke to find himself in occupied Vietnam. Days later, with a select group of fellow laborers (Jerry and a Buddhist South African, escaped just before the overthrow, were the only whites among them), his arm hanging limp and useless at his side, he fought his way across the border into the Republic. Only Jerry made it. The others died and the

South African surrendered. Women soldiers found Jerry wandering beside the Nhi Ha; in his delirium he thought they were American Indians and, when they approached him, turned and began to walk steadily out into the river. (There had been a time when Jerry recoiled from water; now he embraced it, opening his arms to take it to him. A fire in his shoulder.) One of the soldiers crossed herself and dived after him, dragging him by his hair, grown long again now, back to the bank. They took him to their general.

Weeks later, a white face above him, Jerry woke. The light struck his eyes like fists and he quickly shut them again. He heard a voice. English. It sounded far away; it came down long hollow corridors filled with the buzzing of flies.

"Mr. Cornelius?"

Jerry moved his head weakly. There were thorns in his neck, knots of thorns. (Who was it—Schumann? Someone. Dead. Mad, from hearing a constant hum in his ears, and killed himself. A high F. Jerry's was E7, the full chord. In an echo chamber. In his skull.)

"Mr. Cornelius?"

He opened his eyes and shut them even more quickly. They were full of flames.

"You will be all right. My medic——"

Then the buzzing swelled, the flies settled down onto slabs of raw red meat. And then it was inside him, swelling inside him, and it blotted out all the rest.

At night the flames would come back to him, filling the walls of the general's green room. Dark green, deep as the grass at night, bright red and yellow. Among them he could see the faces of his wife and son, Cass and Dylan (Dylan, he thought, Welsh for *water*), their faces black, dissolving, hair afire and eyes staring out at him. Her brown eyes wide, empty, as the fire (or was there fear in them?) picked the flesh off her body and Jerry remembered himself how soft each part would feel to the fire's rough hands. The child would open his mouth, scream, scream, but there would be no sound over the roar of flames and collapsing buildings, only his mouth open round and the flames leaping inside it. Their faces behind the flames now. And then, at the edge of the flames, he would hear the gentle, quick laughter of Michael, his friend. The sound of Michael saying: Guilt.

General Lee was a mercenary—or had been, until he found every regular soldier above him dead or wounded, the other mercenaries crossing the border, and the people here in Haiphong (women, children, the crippled and insane) looking to him for leadership. Secretly, he had made arrangements to leave the country; then the Republic was proclaimed and, inexplicably, supported by the League of Nations. That night a man was found dead in his small boat anchored just off the harbor, and the next day General Lee had assumed official control of the border sector, "Lee County." Weapons were requisitioned, and supplied. They were mostly .22's of American make. In the weeks which followed Lee's assumption, the few South Vietnamese soldiers who crossed into the North, and several mercenaries who tried to return, were quickly shot and torn apart by Lee's squads of women. They had no idea what force hatred, combined with loss and near-Messianic devotion, could have.

The General was small, like the people he "looked after," with slick black hair gathered to one side of his head with a blood-red ribbon. Beneath his thin, sharp face there were only the dense robes, blue, rising high on his neck and dropping over his hands and bare feet, giving no indication whatsoever of a body within them. He was an American, born in Louisiana and escaped just before the revolutions and final secession. He was Cajun, and still spoke with a slight French accent. "The bayous for the rice fields," he would say, the dark blue robes swaying ponderously as he gestured toward the lands beyond the patio. "It was not a difficult exchange."

Jerry remained with the General for several weeks, during which time he was given the best care and medical attention possible to the city, now little more than a village, though all the rubble had been cleared long ago and everything within Haiphong was clean and neatly ordered. The man who cared for him was in fact the General's own specially imported physician, a large, vague man with hands that reminded Jerry of palm leaves, who never spoke and never met Jerry's—or anyone's—eyes. Most likely this meant he was German. Jerry suspected so, but there were few Germans left after the '38 crisis in Ostrava and Jerry, having never seen one, couldn't be sure. "Du är ein Deutsche," he said one day as his bandages were being changed. That was the best he could manage. He knew a little Danish, and he dimly recalled struggling through Rilke as a child, but that was long ago; still, he thought the man would understand. But he made no reaction. He continued unwinding the soiled gauze and cotton, carried it carefully across the tiles to the disposal unit, then took fresh wrappings out of the sterilizer and bound them tightly across Jerry's chest and arm. When he had finished, he turned and left the room. Jerry's shoulder stang where he had pulled the mats of cotton away from the new, forming skin, following it with a gentle pressure of his fingertips to ease the pain.

Though it was rumored he had once been Taoist, the General had no religion, a rare thing these days; Jerry couldn't in fact remember ever having met another person —aside from himself, of course—who had been able to make his way through the welter of ancient and ephemeral codes of belief which the world offered now. The General was an ascetic, however, and this presented something of a problem. Still, love of a sort was possible between them, and in its own way, slowly, that love developed. When Jerry was better, the General sent women to his room several nights in succession. Jerry's turning them away (kindly and, once, regretfully) somehow cemented the relationship between the General and himself. They settled into a smooth, pure love, expressed in the many nights they spent alone together drinking local tea and talking (the General smoking rice-hulls in a briar pipe; this and the tea were the only concessions he allowed himself), fed by one's guilt and the other's gratitude, or by some curious combination of the two which existed in each. Soon they were speaking in French, falling back onto English when Jerry occasionally found the General's distorted Cajun French impenetrable, then onto Mandarin when the divergence of English and American became, as it often did, obtrusive. It was an experience wholly unique for Jerry, like nothing he had ever known or imagined.

The night he left, the General signed a safe passage for

Jerry and escorted him to the boat which was to take him on the first lap toward Calcutta.

The sun was almost down, its maroons and ochres lying out flat along the river, filling it with color. Birds skimmed low to the surface. In the distance their wings, the size of Jerry's hand, appeared to be single feathers and their long legs, dangling down into the clear water, looked like lengths of thin bamboo.

"You'll come back, Mr. Cornelius?" the General asked, in English. His brown eyes were very still, and caught none of the light from the water. It occurred to Jerry that they had never touched.

"Would there be something to come back to, General? When the time came?" From across the city he could hear the sound of gunfire as the women's army practiced on targets. Jerry had seen the targets; they were roughly-drawn outlines of small men, with the heart, genitals and brain carefully drawn in.

"There is only peace here, Mr. Cornelius, and that will not change. Nor will our values. Trouble and strife have done with our land. Now they have gone elsewhere, as you are about to do."

"Calcutta. . . ."

"Perhaps. But not, I think, for the moment."

"And perhaps if I did return, I would bring the wars back with me?"

The General turned and looked out over the river. "It is possible. You are a most exceptional man. But it is not a thing one finds easy to admit."

The boat's motor coughed twice and caught. General Lee held out his hand to give Jerry the safe passage.

"Good-bye then, Mr. Cornelius."

Jerry took the papers and his fingers for just a moment touched the General's palm. Impulsively he reached out to the blue robes, then dropped his hand. "I—" He turned and jumped quickly into the boat. Only when it was far out on the water and Jerry looked back to see the General standing there alone on the harbor did he begin to cry.

He was still weeping when the boat docked at Haing Nhu Khan.

The burning city. Brown eyes. An open soundless mouth.

Jerry lay on one of the Persian carpets, staring into the empty fireplace. The words, remembered, were inside him: guilt, loss, denial, fear. Guilt. Michael's words, above the burning city.

It was all locked in his childhood. London, Simla. But wasn't the house, London—

Gone. It was no use; Jerry was confused. ("My childhood bends beside me. Too far for me to lay a hand there once or lightly.") There seemed so many childhoods when he tried to recall them, and all of them gone. Perhaps there was one for every change his body had suffered, the world filled with the broken childhoods of Jerry Cornelius. If that were true. . . .

It would all be over soon.

London, Simla, now Calcutta, Mashhad. He had to get it all outside him; that was the only way.

Anything.

He tried to shake his head but the movement wasn't right. He knew what he meant to do but, for several moments, the words wouldn't come. This sort of thing had happened quite a lot recently; Jerry suspected he was suffering aphasia—slight, but on several levels. Words eluded him, almost there, the concept firm but the words would fail to congeal around it, would be inaccurate, distorted. Other times, the words themselves would evoke no response. His gestures, too, were impaired, contradictory or at best inadequate.

He squeezed his right hand hard into a fist and managed to regain control. He rolled over in the carpet and got up, walking toward a small shelf of books beside the fireplace. He ran his finger slowly along the books, stopped at one, slid the finger up along the spine and tilted it out. He took it down, turning it over and over in his hands, the stiff coolness of it.

It was a small, thin volume, Foolscap 16mo, bound in black. The spine was bare. *Abyssinia,* in deep blue on the front. And below, in tiny silver letters: *Jeremiah Cornelius.* (Once he had refused a Nobel Prize for his unified-field theory; this time, he was saved such embarrassment. The night before publication he had broken into the printer's warehouses and burned every copy of the book, then methodically searched out every pre-release copy and disposed of it. This, to the best of his knowledge, was the sole remaining copy now, after the city's burning.) He opened the book, at random, saw first lines and had no need to read further. He remembered.

The murder

> I shall never,
> never kill you, no. You will always
> be there
> on the headstone of morning;

your name
is written under my pillow on the walls,
the bottom of the toilet lid,

the towels. Your face
is inside all the spoons.

Living with you

Another year and the ground
pulls harder,
the heart
on its intricate stalk succumbs again
to your hair, your breath and voice.
A tree
grows, and the world grows
smaller. A pan on the stove,
boiling too much water,
raises the level of entropy in the world.

He didn't want to look at the dedication, but had to. It
was in 6pt Perpetua, almost lost to the creamy white of
the page.

To Camus,
who had no childhood;
To Dylan,
who will have nothing else;
and Cass.

He was sixteen, married, happy, and afraid. "A man of
independent means." There had been this, a novel called
Moth ("Father, the dark moths/ Crouch at the sills of

earth, waiting"—from James Wright), then the scientific
treatises destroyed with his father's house, the unified-
field theory (Who? Someone had told him, "It was your
chance of immortality—you may never have another"),
and then . . .

Jerry began to cry.

The epigraph was on the page opposite the dedication,
in Tempo, bold small capitals. Camus. "There is only one
liberty, to come to terms with death. After which, everything is possible." His voice soft, damp and choked, Jerry
read it aloud. When he finished, the words remained in
the room.

He looked around at the bare walls, the matched Persian
carpets, the colonial cane furniture he'd brought here.
The fireplace he never used. Her painting above it: soft-
bodied women in groups, bleak, with hollow mouths and
weak orange hair. Christ, he thought. Christ. It was true.
Everything was water if you looked long enough.

He was still crying, but the tears helped now.

—Sorry to bother you, General Cornelius, but New
Olgayte is bombing us again.

—Where the hell is New Olgayte?

—That new South American republic, sir. The one

—Oh, them. Again! With our own goddamn bombs, I
suppose.

—Yes sir. What should we do, sir?

—Do? Don't be an ass, Brunner, you know we can't do
anything. They'll get tired and stop eventually. More
likely run out of missiles in an hour or so, anyhow.

—They've wiped out Denver, Louisiana's hit bad. Most

of the Midwest. Mexico too, but we think that was a
miscalculation.

—You've got to admire the little bastards.

—Yes sir.

Jerry was walking through the Mashhad streets, his
light-weight black boots pushing through the mud and
garbage, his fine black hair flapping behind him like a tiny
cape. He was wearing a scarlet Edwardian suit that made
his face look even paler than usual. He hadn't eaten for
weeks, and was thinning back down from the influence of
General Lee's rich food and drink.

The architecture here—baroque cotyledon pods looped
and grooved with gold, occasional jade, makeshift concrete bunkers left from the war and taken over by the new
government, wooden-slat houses—suited Jerry's mood
perfectly. It was March, it had been raining for five days,
and now it was very hot. Sweat gathered in Jerry's thick
eyebrows, ran down his back inside the clothing. It collected, also, in his rough new mariner's beard. He took the
clay pipe out of his mouth in sudden disgust and threw it
onto the street, then immediately wished he hadn't. The
smell was terrible.

The markets were closed and no one else was about. A
pack of dogs came out of one of the houses, spotted Jerry,
and went running off together down the street away from
him; only one stayed behind, nuzzling at the garbage and
snorting as water went up its nose. One of its legs was
chewed almost to the bone. Jerry had been locked away
inside his house for some time. He had no way of knowing
why the people had left the city—or, indeed, if they all

had. He noticed that there were no flies. On one of the bunkers a wet flag sagged against the pole. Like the buildings it was curiously hybrid, stillborn. In the center of a grass-green field an orange lion stood facing left, a sword in its paw. Yellow words in Farsi—probably a Sunni slogan—spilled out of its mouth. Behind it, a fierce red sun emblem raged, diminishing the rest.

Jerry passed close to a doorway and felt a pressure on his shoulder. He looked down and saw a ruined brown hand, looked back up and saw an old woman standing there. Her teeth were gone, the lips and skin around them little more than loose, leather-like flaps. She had been fat once, but now there was no flesh under the skin, and it had fallen into sags, slack and baggy like ancient breasts, covering her face. Which was probably just as well. He shouldn't have liked to see what was in that face. One ear was torn off, the eye on the same side half-closed and running; the thick gray fluid had dried in several of the creases down that side of her face, weeks or months old. The bones were bending, fusing, pulling the body in toward them. She was naked, and her hand trembled on Jerry's shoulder. Even in the garbage-filled street, she stank.

"Jerry," the old woman said. She spoke in Kurdish. "Don't you know me?" He could barely make out the words—pick them out of the mumbling—but he knew. Her hair was still violent red.

"Miss Brunner! Why, I haven't seen you since——"

"No. You haven't." She pulled the hand away and it fell limply to her side. She raised her head, and that seemed to take all the strength she had left. "I've missed you, Jerry."

"Aristophanes and all that?"

"*Like* that, yes. I've changed, haven't I, Jerry?"

Jerry was full—of contempt or impatience, he wasn't sure which.

"Not significantly, Miss Brunner." Contempt, then.

"Ah, but I have, Jerry, and so have the times. Things get back to normal so quickly."

"Normal? My God——"

"Change requires death and destruction, Jerry. And change is normal."

"'We are conceived in our conceits.'" Jerry shook his head. "No. You haven't changed. That's the same old Miss Brunner saying that."

Suddenly she stood up straight and almost made a smile out of the flaps of skin around her mouth. "We stopped too soon, Mr. Cornelius."

"We didn't stop, Miss Brunner. We were stopped."

She collapsed again, her arms hanging out in front of the stooped body. She looked down and closed her eyes. Finally she said, "In the East. It was the East, wasn't it, Jerry? They stopped us in the East."

"Kuwait. We didn't get even that far."

She was quiet for several minutes. The dog started hesitantly toward them and Jerry kicked out at it, spattering muck against its side. It turned and ran away, limping and, a little farther on, falling. It didn't get back up. Jerry could hear it whimpering.

"Have you read Firbank, Miss Brunner?" he said, impulsively. "Firbank feared that serious talk would always become sober tosh. Firbank was right."

"There is a word . . ."

"Rodomontade. There are always words, Miss Brunner."

"Yes." That seemed to be the last of her breath.

"But we should have that one tattooed on our chests."

He turned and started away but the hand, somehow, managed to get to his shoulder again.

"Jerry. I've missed you, Jerry. Where are you staying?"

He grinned. "Hilton."

She shrugged her body down out of the doorway into the street. He thought for a moment she was going to fall, like the dog.

"That's a lie, Jerry." She stared away from him down the street.

"Yes. Of course."

She began to walk away, ponderously dragging her feet through the clogged, clotted streets, dragging the legs and then the body above them. She would die, he thought, unless she found someone soon.

"Good-bye, Miss Brunner."

"It's 'Mrs.' now. Good-bye, Mr. Cornelius."

Jerry stood watching her walk away. She reached a corner and turned, staggering against one of the bunkers. She rested a few seconds, then pushed herself back upright and went on. Jerry realized he was muttering to himself—

> *Out of the ash*
> *I rise with my red hair*
> *And I eat men like air.*

He shivered, and a tear ran down the crease of his cheek into the corner of his mouth. He reached up and brushed the hair back away from his face, felt the wetness on his fingertips now. He went over to the whimpering dog, raised a foot, and crushed its skull with the heel of his boot. It never moved.

The next day, he left the city.

He searched the house methodically. He went through every drawer, every cupboard, gutted all the furniture. He opened the back of the toilet and let out the water. He pulled off ventilators. He climbed to look down into light fixtures. He rapped on the walls, the floor. He took the tops off the stairs. He blew both safes—nothing but gold. He looked up the chimney—never used. He paced off the floors, walked outside and paced along the sides of the house. Nothing.

It wasn't here.

The floor was already covered with stuffing, rattling paper, splinters and slabs of wood, bricks, plaster. Furious, he tore the colonial cane furniture apart and threw it across the room. He ripped up the rugs with a knife from the kitchen. He dumped the books onto the floor and smashed the bookcase against a wall. After that it was more difficult, but he did what he could.

Finally he stood at the door and looked back, pleased.

There. That would give the bastard something to think about.

He was going to die.

There was a cable waiting for him when he reached his house off Holland Park Avenue. There were also quite a lot of newspapers. He caught a glimpse of the headline on top of the four-foot stack, a *Daily Mail: Sadistic Skipper Drowns Parrot.* Chuckling, he opened the yellow envelope.

He had cabled, "What is the exact nature of the catastrophe. Don't know. Don't know. Back soon." And Michael answered, *Another collaboration, Jerry?* (Jerry and his wife had referred to the birth of Dylan as a collaboration; did his friend know this?) *I love you. I miss you.*

Another collaboration . . . yes. But with whom—Michael? There wasn't enough of Michael left. Miss Brunner? He didn't know where she was, even if she was alive, after Kuwait. The General, the girl?

Then he noticed the last line of Michael's cable. *Come home. I fear for your life, Jerry.* He went inside and began to laugh, and went on laughing, insanely, wildly, beyond control, until he was out of breath—then collapsed among the wreckage, still laughing, rolled over and passed out.

They lay side by side, on their backs, in the bed. His heart beat irregularly; he put his hand over it and watched the fingers being pushed away from his chest. The fingers were pleasantly thin.

Aside from the bed, a framework of hollow brass tubing and a mattress, there were only two low bamboo tables in the room. On one of them lay a small two-stringed instrument with a gourd body. On the other there were teacups without handles which would fit perfectly inside cupped hands, an alcohol burner, a loaf of ricecake. The windows were bare. Outside, a tear-shaped . . . kite. That was the word. (The aphasia again?) A tear-shaped white kite with a short white tail drifted steadily, slowly, across the cloudless sky. The afternoon sun showed on the side of one sill and the wall opposite. Outside, it would be hot; here everything was cool, even her body beside him.

"You're rather sentimental, Mr. Cornelius."

"Yes, I know. Hell, isn't it?"

He reached out, very gently, and touched the bruise on her thigh, laying two fingers on the aureola. (He was amazed at his capacity for tenderness now, this moment.) It was beautiful. Almost perfectly round. There were three distinct colors, with bits of rainbow hue between them. The center very small, a spot of deep blue the size of the pupil of an eye and almost as dark; then the aureola of purple-brown, like another color for skin; a narrow penumbra outside, brown becoming yellow—and then the smooth whiteness of her skin. Her body was familiar to him, almost painfully so.

"You don't mind, then?" he asked.

She sat up and tossed the short brown hair back away from her face. Her eyes, too, were brown. Her breasts were so small they hardly moved; they were little more than the large, still puckered nipples. Her stomach rubbed against her thighs as she shook her head.

"Names don't matter, Mr. Cornelius. They are only words, and they mean nothing. Only gestures matter, between people." She watched the kite as it began to bounce, riding the corridors of wind. "That is all we can ask of another. My last . . . the last man I was with. He would have me take emetics before sex. When I climaxed —" She looked back at Jerry and grinned. "And sometimes he would join me."

"Without benefit of the emetics, I suppose?"

"Yes." She touched his hand, which was still lying gently across the bruise. "He put that there, at first. But I thought it was beautiful, and I wanted to keep it. Every few days it begins to fade and then I——"

"This man. It was in London? I think I know him."

"I believe you do." She rolled to get a cigarette and Jerry's hand slid off her leg. The breeze was steady now. The kite throbbed on its string, a cloud behind it. It began to rain, and the kite struggled as it was pulled toward the ground. Rain spattered on the sill. Jerry lay quietly for several minutes and watched the rain, the new water. (Dylan, he thought. Dylan was another word for water.) The girl sat beside him smoking. Hash, from the smell. He studied the casual white symmetry of her back, amazed at it.

"Words," he said after a while. "Mallarmé said that poetry was made from words, not ideas." (That had come to him, he had remembered that, as he sat with Michael on the hill above the burning city.)

"French? Yes, it would take a Frenchman to say that. But I didn't think anyone knew French anymore."

"I've been to America," Jerry said. "Louisiana. And long before that . . ."

She waited for him to go on. When he didn't, she took the last drags of the hash into her lungs, held them, and said, "At any rate, it's true now." She exhaled, coughing slightly, then rolled on her buttocks and took a meer-schaum-colored ceramic ashtray off the floor. She stubbed the cigarette out with deliberate concentration, squeezing the filter together and pushing down till the end crumpled like a drinking-straw wrapper. When she took her hand away, the end was smashed into the ashtray, the rest angled, tip tilted thirty degrees or so up from the bottom. (The associations, Jerry thought. They're starting again.) The filter was oval now, and there was a thin line of stain across it. It looked like a tiny mouth, precise and perfect as the fingernails of a newborn child. The kite was gone from the window.

"Do you know the work of Mirosłav Hołub, Mr. Cornelius? He is a countryman of mine, a Czech. In 'The Root
of the Matter' he wrote,

> There is poetry in everything. That
> is the biggest argument
> against poetry."

"No. The Russians . . ."

"Yes. The Russians. I suppose the world hated us for
that. Still, we had much to lose, either way. We cannot all
be as fortunate as the Americans; we can't all remain
neutral for fifty years. Look at Switzerland. The world
hates them, too."

"The world recovered, dear. It was a little more
drained, a little whiter, but the world always recovers. It
has an amazing capacity for muddling on through."
(Damn Firbank, he thought. Damn him for being right.)
"Things can be destroyed only when they have some
value. Or values." Enough, then, of that. Jerry got up and
began to dress. He noticed a tiny red sore, an eruption,
like a pimple, on his penis. He shrugged and pulled on the
scarlet suit, sat on the bed and pushed his feet into the
boots, still filthy from Mashhad. He stood and turned
back to the girl.

"I'll find him in London, then?"

She nodded.

"Why are you telling me this?"

She paused, her pale face tilted to one side, staring at
him. The nipples were relaxed now, small orange cylin-
ders against her flat chest. The lipstick glistened slightly.
"Perhaps . . . perhaps it is because I am sentimental too,
Mr. Cornelius."

Jerry went across the room and opened the door. "I'll see you again. Soon."

She smiled. "Be discreet, Mr. Cornelius."

"Thank you, but I'd rather be dead."

"Good-bye then, Mr. Cornelius."

Jerry went out, closing the door gently behind him. Out into the rain. Where the thin fabric was soon soaked and it looked like blood.

The door was heavy teak. Grooves had been cut into it and filled with bronze, resembling the whorls and veins of various leaves. When he knocked, it opened and a slender, tall man stood there blinking. The room was dark behind him, dark and warm. He wore scarlet trousers and a bright yellow shirt. The top button was undone, the broad flowered tie tugged partly away from his neck. His black hair was fine, falling onto his shoulders. His face was pale, his mouth ascetic.

"You're Cornelius?" He pushed his way in and shut the door. The man backed quietly away and made no move to resist.

"Yes . . ." Then he smiled and said, "Yes. I've been expecting you." He raised his hand and pushed the hair together behind his neck. It had just been washed; it was still a bit wet, and it stood slightly out from his head. There was a copy of *Farewell, My Lovely* spread open, face down, on the bed. The pillow was damp where his head had been, the orange bedspread vaguely hollowed from his body.

"Yes, I suppose you have, haven't you." He took the

revolver out of his pocket. It was an American make, a .32 built on a .45 frame, the only one of its kind.

"I see you found your gun."

Yes, he had, finally, in an empty house in Mashhad. After a great deal of searching.

"And you didn't."

"Yes. I believe that puts you one up."

"Six, actually. Since you're counting."

Instinctively, the man backed against the desk. They stood for several minutes staring at one another, smiling. Then one of them stopped.

"Justice," Jerry said, very slowly. "Freedom. Truth. Love." With each word he moved his finger gently against the hair-trigger and the other's body jerked back against the desk, his back arching, as the bullets slapped into him and their soft heads spread like tiny hands across his skin and penetrated.

"Words—" he said, and died for them. His body rolled and fell forward onto the desk, then slid slowly backwards off it. He dropped onto the floor, sat there looking at the window with dim eyes, and finally collapsed against the side of the desk. Very slowly, his shoulder moved toward the corner, downwards, into open space. His head dragged against the edge of the desktop, bent without resistance, and he hit the floor, lying halfway under the desk, staring up at it.

Jerry went over and looked at him for the last time, then reached down and closed his eyes. There was chewing gum stuck all over the bottom of the desktop. Now they were both smiling again. Things were back to normal.

Jerry looked around. There was nothing else in the

room but the book and the coat that matched the trousers. It was hung on the back of a reading chair. He walked over and checked the pockets, taking out the safe passage stamped *Republic of Vietnam* and signed *General Lee,* which was all they contained. There was probably money and identification in the trousers, but Jerry had no use for either.

"Good-bye, Mr. Cornelius," he said. He supposed it was bound to happen sooner or later. He went into the hall and shut the door behind him. It was like advancing to the next chamber of a nautilus. The lights were very bright.

" 'I fear those big words which make us so unhappy,' " Jerry said for the dead man.

There was one thing remaining.

Jerry returned to his house off Holland Park Avenue and searched through the rubble and mess the dead man had left behind. Finally he found it at the bottom of a heap of papers and stuffing. He threw it into the fireplace, piling loose paper and stuffing on top of it—madly, frenzied—until the fireplace was filled. Then he struck a match, held it a moment and tossed it in. The pile caught at once, bursting into flame with a sound like that of the wind, expanding, all the bits exploding away from one another.

Jerry stood watching. Balls of burning paper and cotton wool rolled out into the room and he kicked them back. The flames, the poems, rose gently into the chimney.

That night Jerry dreamed of the burning city. Buildings tumbled back into themselves, pushing the flames higher through the empty corridors; people stood still in the harbor and stared; bodies and rubble and refuse drifted on the black waters toward him; and then there was only the fire, in the water, in the buildings—only the flames. But the woman and the child were no longer there inside them, and he wasn't sure now what the flames meant.

By morning the American planes were overhead. The bombs falling slowly, slowly, tumbling down into London. . . .

When the first ones struck, Jerry was thinking of the girl, the kite, the fingernails of a newborn child.

⚙ IV ⚙

Occasions

Negotiation

DUST inhabits the universe. You walk across a plain that was once a sea, and you sink to your knees in the dust. As fine and light as flour, as the ash of dead leaves, and brown. Behind, the dust is already filling your steps, your legs. The trees are gone, the plain is barren. Bare. Only here and there, spaced yards apart, brittle flowers with their stems wrapped round the heart of the world, which crumble to dust at your touch. The same color as the dust. And other places, places where the still unmoving sun has gratuitously focused its stale heat, where the dust has swelled or collapsed, spotting and pocking the earth. Aside from this, nothing breaks the level brown which extends to the horizon like a now-lifeless and limp band of elastic. A plane.

NOTHING . . . but a single stone. Again and again you have traversed this plain, this world; and all that remains is this solitary stone, perfectly smooth and round. White? Of course. And if you touch it? It will crumble, be cool to your hand; the sun will resume its motion and flowers burst forth out of the suddenly firm ground; slowly outwards from the rock the dust will fade to water, shadows and then their trees appear; the brittle flowers lengthen and grow together, twine together, turning green to cover the dust in depths of moss; blood drain into the sky and blotch the day with orange and settle to violet and then to purple; the rock split open and expel a thousand gaping fish, or the fish's round mouths—

WHAT? And if I lay my hand in the scarce shade of the rock, could I retrieve it? The shade? Or the hand? Could I cup the shade within my hands and lay it, hold it, against my face? Would the hand take root and grow there like a mushroom, first engine of life for these plains, this new world. . . .

MOVING away from the stone, over the brown expanse, you are hardly surprised to find that your legs fail to re-emerge from the dust and that the stumps, visible behind you as cavities, are filling and brimming over with water. Or acid: a lake, a sea. A shore?

Dédicaces

1.

I fear I am coming apart.

Last night as I made to turn over in my bed, one arm cracked away. I looked back to where it remained asleep and calm on the sheet; to the seam, as yet indistinct, forming along it. And this morning when I seated myself here, that part of the legs below the knee dropped on to the floor like pieces of firewood—when I lifted my pen the shoulder burst open and small bubbles of sound tumbled out to break themselves open, striking against the room's objects—I attempted to return to that arm in the bedroom—

But no; how can I hope to describe it? the experience of watching from eyes yards apart (the first secure beneath a shelf, the other under a foot's next step), one disengaged hand moving across the paper.

2.

His hand blunders through another morning. The man with no more past. "My lead soles hold me erect and slow, grotesque, I advance, choked by this collar, and lean awkwardly over the marsh-like lives of women."

Comme un escargot le soleil à travers le dôme du ciel commence sa journée. Et la dame. A côte.

[You asked for a poem and the best I could do was . . . the best I could do. And last night—born in ourselves; that single moment—an illusion to prove you don't exist. Today the hand that tries to touch you holds warm space. The pages of my notebook, arrachées.]

He lifts his arm into the noose of light from the window, which falls in a line along his wrist. The hand severed. Decapitated. He laughs, waking the girl.

That night, in Orion's cold palm, like a torch it will reappear.

Event

They are moving the city again. For the third time this year the men arrive in their trucks and brown trousers, smiling. They drive their vehicles wildly like Dodgem Cars among, into, against the buildings. Walls, windows, doors fall into the back of the trucks and the trucks begin to move away, out of the city; to take them somewhere else. The remains are washed away by torrential rains, which follow.

31 December 3 A.M.

The great vacant space permits it.

Go on, put out your hand. Touch it, warmly. The beat of the blood in your hand, feel, the separate heat of each finger. In your hand it is smaller. It can't draw back; it is surrounded by sky.

You've walked the path backwards, arms to the east and west. You have a right to know, to this. Moss splits the hump of your back, your left leg like a cat's moves ahead of itself; your tongue licks stains from the air as you speak to trees or whatever is within them, what they contain. The questions you ask.

Left behind, with what I can never say: what you've left behind. I hold the air in my hands and wish for wind, le vent de ma mer, the winds of the wing of madness. But never, never what I want to say (memory, the hunting horn, that dies along the wind). The roofs ascend to the lowest rays of the sun, no higher. The afternoon is a space.

The hour. The pause between your steps, the expanse from finger to finger. There are spaces between your breath, the bee's song, the drop of blood from auricle to ventricle, these words and letters; the page, my eyes. Even between the pen and page, a minute space. Dust and sand the emblems of this, that winds will fill.

But the great vacant space allows it. Victory, or possession. Yours; take it; it has no place else to go.

Inside you. Held down by the weight of years.

The space admits it. We are all the space, the space between things, the space does not contain us. We inhabit ourselves. Take it inside yourself. . . .

"And I fill my hands with your tears."

Retrouvé

I watched the leaf stand up and walk back to the tree,
   climb up the trunk. It went out along a branch; paused;
   then into the confusion of limbs and tiny twigs. Decided on one and settled there, very still.
It has done this several times now and I am still watching.

Procés

Another morning, another joyless celebration.
The grass is burning. The crow weighs its stillness on the
   limb. With my eye in the sun.
And at the window in the knives of the mirror you are
   watching.

Another morning and I am looking into myself. The un-
filled space around a man.
Women, then. And further nameless disconnections.
Cloud upon cloud and it darkens. Five years of it, five
more, and my hand become something I don't recognise.
"The hand leaves the clay and is red."
So that's what I am.
In the presence of bone, a man closing up. And between
the words growing old.

Menstruum

He used to do things like that. Stand at the top of hills,
jump up into the sky and grab a handful of it. Not even
breathing hard, "There, see, you're not real at all."
He used to make fun of the horizon like that.
Now it's got him.

❀ ❀ ❀ ❀ ❀

A marriage

You always preferred, I remember, even then,
the ridge of the eyes. Washington
was your favorite—the high
forehead, the nose like a flat fish—

and for me it was Lincoln.
The cheekbone arc de triomphe,
the jaw a cheap couch-shape
and the cheeks sunk just enough

to push back into and sit there.

Our shoes bit into the upper lip
and we tiptoed to put our arms up into
the nostrils, where a hard liver-colored

fungus was growing, we reached
and finally broke off
one small piece. You carried it

from my palm to your lips. They
opened slowly, shut. Closed
around it. It was good;

savory and nourishing. We took more,
and more, until both were filled. . . .

And now we sleep in ears, eyes,
where teeth should be—curled up
under the lines of lips, each asleep
in the hammock of an eyelid.

The mushrooms are yellow now,
and your hair turns color before
the seasons, pulling them along.
Nothing moves below us; and above,

nothing but the seasons, years
passing. The city has been moved. Our trips down
across the front of the face grow
more rare every week now. We

hate the days, descent
of any sort. We have filled our shoes up

with peace. We are growing thin.
Like the birds who used to come here.

The faces are smeared, blurred with dust.
Below, the sand and gravel of
eyes, cheeks, noses, eyes,
where teeth should be. We are content.

9 below 0

Today a man died on the street. They say
the bullets spread their soft hands
          across his skin like words
and urged it open. Collapsing off the stone
          side of the building
where the loud gun had thrown him,
a corridor appeared in him all at once,
          the size
of a nearby manhole. He gave birth to a vacuum,
that sucked his bowels out onto the street
          near Macy's.
The wall behind him slammed by a huge red fist;
          pebbles, plaster,
falling into him. The manager calls the police,
          an ambulance,
and then the workmen. They can come tomorrow.

Today a man died on the street. They say
it was terrible. It makes the evening headlines;
          TV coverage
shows him lying inside himself on the sidewalk,
          dead, the people
in crowded rings watching. And him, the other
          (they say

he was like that for an hour), standing still
    with the gun
limp in his hand, and smiling.

Today a man died on the street. At Broadway
    and 34th,
3 p.m. on a warm day, the 3rd of December—
but what of it? Why all this bother?

Just that one man is empty
and done with listening to others; and another
finally found a way to speak, to say
all the things he wanted, dumb for years.

A vid

Heads down, and the torch blinking
Along the sand, we follow. Here the tracks
Of feet with claws, disparallel lines
Sliding away and back on either side,
Like an exhausted polygraph. The batteries are old,
Dimming. Our breath, the fog
Gather towards the torch. And there,
Beside and behind them,
The path of something else, something
Like limp, trailing wings.

And now, ahead in the darkness,
There is a click, as of
Chambers revolving all together to the next
Warm corridor, beetles closing
On wings
In the carapace, coffin cases. The torch

Stammers, flashes. Flares. Dies. In your hand
Now, it is itself
Something else.

Gauge

I'm so tired of it, the women with trees
Between their legs, the forest of possible eductions.
And the stork riding his ridiculous red roses
Towards us across the desert again.

> the tracks progressing well
> cable, Ready soon, rails laid on time
> the locomotive will

Red needles swing across the face of our days, leaving red
Behind. Mensurate, commiserate. Anacoluthon—hearing
Delicious lips open inside a morning. The giraffes' snake-like
Heads silent above the trees.

> commensurate, comminution, commisure

And the silver threads dashing along the cobalt seams,
Day. The comity of nations continues, allows us to remain
Here. Horizons appear at intervals. Then the work stops;
An ostrich comes to borrow water from our tanks.

> and other manifestations of length, duration
> the absence of ants, flies, inchworms
> the moths crouched waiting

Insects desert the sun in a line from the horizon, in single
File. Gracchus laughs and watches each queue and wait its
Turn. He names them. Another cable, Rails almost done

Trees down No more Please cable return Further
Instructions.

the horizons vanish

Feet among ties, even the giraffes are waiting. We release
The construction into the landscape. It scatters,
Correcting the sand's pronunciation; it lies under the sun
In articulate fragments, random as facts. Someone applauds.

"there was no other choice"
"but within it lie other choices"
the cable unanswered

The insects pause, then march one by one into the aardvark's
Dead mouth—and tumble
In knots from the eyes. We wait, and watch.

What to do tomorrow

When the whistles and sirens
blow, go
quietly to your study.

You will have time enough.
It has all been planned; there will be
a ten-minute lull
before the fire and fog horns begin.
That is the final sign.
It must all be orderly.

Leave a note concerning
how you feel; the few
that survive could be useful.

Pile books against the windows
and walls.
Use the thickest ones you have
and pack as many there as you have
time for.

Pull a table into one corner.
Situate youself under it and
stack more of them
around you, until you
are encased in a kind of igloo.

Tests have proved them to be
as effective as sandbags. Wait for the
all-clear. This will be
one long blow of the horns

followed by the sirens
and factory whistles again.
Sit in there thinking

how you always wondered
what they were for.

❀   ❀   ❀   ❀   ❀

Les amis

A large London department store. It is an extremely old
building, renovated countless times, and covers most of the
block. Above the new pastel façade an old legend remains, Royal Academy of Artists in Watercolour, near the

top of the building and just below the cornice, chiseled out in letters which are four inches high and protrude from the worn gray stone almost a full inch. There are two double-size revolving doors at the front and a side entrance some twenty feet wide, wholly open to the street. Above and below this orifice, air issues from fans to form an invisible curtain retaining interior heat, impervious to external cold; passing through it one feels a momentary warm tingle, like a dandelion run across the skin of the face. Windows run the length of the building at both sides—clothing, stationery, toiletry, household appliances and culinary apparatus composed behind them as carefully as in Flemish paintings. The glass is five inches thick; yet there is no distortion, no imperfection in these forty thousand solid inches, two thousand pounds, of glass.

An old man, shabbily dressed in clothes from Portobello Road, has been walking from door to door, window to window along the block for some time, his face floating in the dishes and silver utensils of the window. He looks closely at each person who emerges from the store alone. And if you broke those black eyes open on the pavement there might be, deep at the centre, the last dying spark of a fire.

After a while a man but slightly younger than he—dressed, however, in the finest clothes, like those in the windows alongside which the old man has lived for so long—stepped through one of the doors (at no point did any part of the door touch him) and began walking with determination down the pavement, no doubt to some appointment or business engagement.

A dime, the old man said as he passed. To buy a friend?

The other turned towards him and stopped. Sun glistened in his silver hair and he smiled—he could see his own smile in the window behind the beggar.

They're all out, he said. I was just in, myself. Thought it would make a nice gift you understand.

All out, you say.

I'm afraid so. Terribly sorry. I know how it is, but there's not a single one left, in the entire store. I had hoped . . . He shook his head and the smile came back. You really should be inside you know, not out on the streets. Weather like this. He reached under his coat and brought out a tooled-leather wallet. Sold out. Completely. And not even noon yet. The season I guess, the rush. He handed the old man a five pound note. Come back next time—buy yourself a whole family, a party, anything you want. They're planning another sale in a fortnight or so, I believe. Come back then. He began to walk away.

Not even a return, a second-hand one?

Nothing, the man said, walking on down the street.

Nothing. . . .

He watched the man's back until it turned away from him around a corner. Then he himself started down the block, the block he knew so well, past all the windows and the curtains of warm air towards the park.

He sat on a bench and watched. All the people were walking in pairs. A young couple were listening to the radio on the ground between them. A speaker was saying to a small crowd, We must come together. And all around the old man pigeons stirred and settled, like dark thoughts in the afternoon sun.

After a while the money fell from his hand and began to tumble and somersault out across the grass and cement and flowers of the park. Like just another leaf, and there were so many trees. None of the walking couples noticed; though some time later a child could be seen far away, skipping after it. Alone.

Winner

We're going in at the same time and only one of us is going to come back out. Ten in the morning. No dinner tonight, no breakfast. It's all set. I've told him that but he won't believe it. He just lies there groaning every few minutes saying We're gonna make it Joe, we're both gonna make it. And then a fit of coughing hits him and the nurse comes running.

Three, four times a day Bill goes through the ward taking the bets. They've picked up a lot in the last week or so. More of them, and higher—the coughs and the special nurse, I guess. There's only one guy in the ward now who hasn't kicked in, and we finally figured out he was deaf. Every night just before lights-out Bill comes round to tell me how much is in the pot. When he brings the pills. It's up to $348.83 now. Not bad. I've done worse on the outside in my day, a lot worse.

Bill's a grad student at Columbia in Black Studies. He's on scholarship, maybe a grant or two, but he's working nights as an orderly to help finance his Panther block. He's got light skin and fine features and he could pass for white a lot of places I know. But he's not too happy about that. So he wears an Afro and comes on pretty strong. First day I was here, back about a month ago, he told me he was black maybe four or five times. Nothing direct. Just a word here and there, an aside, like that.

The guy next to me. He's a little guy. Pushes a hack, and he got torn up pretty bad by two young negroes up near Harlem. They brought him in about a week ago and it looked like he wasn't going to make it for a while there, but they stuck some tubes in him and he had needles all in his arm the first two, three days and they had him under an oxygen tent. Bill used to go over and stick his head inside and breathe deep as he could, then he'd come back with a big grin on him. Anyhow, they had to wait this long for him to get his strength back, like with me. When he came to and saw the orderly was black they almost lost him again and assigned a special nurse to him. First thing he said that day, and he wasn't talking to anyone, was, I been shoving that damn cab for fifteen years now, I oughta know better. He doesn't talk much, I don't know if he can, but there's something about him I like. One thing is he's got guts, he's tough. You can see that when the pain hits him and he clenches his teeth, holding on. He's not the kind that gives up easy—it's a long way from the Bronx, but he'll never forget it. And I like that, I know how it is myself.

Right before lights-out tonight Sanders comes over. He makes sure to wait till Bill's gone first, though. They don't have much use for each other, I don't think they even talk. Sanders never got through high school. He had to come up the hard way. And then there's the whole black thing of course. Seems a couple of his buddies on the force got gunned down by the Panthers a year or so back and he can't forget that, not for a minute. But he's a good guy. He knows what's going on, all about the pot Bill's holding I mean, and he's not doing anything about it, won't let it get out.

He stands by the bed a while looking around the ward,

then asks how I'm doing tonight. I grunt and shove the cigarettes toward him. They won't let me smoke but I like to keep the cigarettes around anyhow, I like to know they're there. And I don't figure he needs an answer, he knows I'm slated for tomorrow morning. That means he'll either stick around or pull down another assignment, maybe go back on the beat. But I think he's got a promotion coming up now so who knows. It's sure to be a lot better than this.

I light the cigarette for him and he thanks me and stands there smoking. Finally he says, "You're looking pretty good."

"I'm okay."

He takes another drag and a little smoke comes back out.

"Sorry I had to shoot, Vic. Mayor told us we had to crack down on the rackets. You know what that means. It means the little guys like you, not where it's really at. Order comes down though, not much I can do about it, right?"

"Yeah, sure. Just aim better next time, okay?"

He smiles and looks around again. I don't know what he thinks he's looking for. He knows every crack in the wall by now. "You need anything? Anything I can get you?"

"Yeah, I could use a lung and maybe a kidney. If you've got a spare."

He looks at me while he's snubbing the cigarette out in the bedpan.

"I don't have anything against you, Vic. You're straight. You never gave us any trouble like a lot of the others did. You know that."

"Yeah. I know, Sanders."

"Look. When the trial comes up. I just want you to know I'm on your side. I'll be pulling for you all the way."

"Great. We can say it was a hunting accident. I forgot to wear my red cap. How's that?"

He's watching my face very closely. "I'll do what I can, Vic."

I just nod and he finally says, "Right." He can't think of anything else to say. So he starts away, but I stop him.

"Sanders . . ."

"Yes."

"Do me a favor?"

"Sure, Vic. Anything. You know that."

"Ask Bill to come back in here for a minute. I have to see him."

"Bill . . . ? Yeah. Yeah, sure. Why not." He starts away again and stops, turns around. "Hey. Thanks for the smoke, Vic."

"Anytime. Thanks for the slug." But I'm grinning for him. He goes out through the door and he's gone for a few minutes. Then I see him coming back and he takes up his post just outside the door, in a folding chair out there. A minute or two later Bill comes in. God knows where Sanders might have found him this time of night.

I cut him off before he says anything: "Got something for you, Bill." I reach around under the pillow, take out the roll and hand it to him. The bandages get in the way and it takes a while. "That'll make it about five hundred." When he looks back up at me I shake my head. "No questions." What the hell, there's no one else to give it to.

Bill stares at the money for a moment, then at me. He takes out a little notebook and makes an entry. He knows how to do it right. I could have used a man like him. Then he puts the money in his pocket and leaves. He doesn't say anything to me but I notice he stops outside and talks to Sanders for a minute, maybe two. Sanders turns around in his chair and glances at me.

I think I was right about the promotion.

Residue

During the writing of his famous critique of contemporary art, *Estimations* (a work comprising but 96 pages yet, despite the author's incapacity for any language other than English, quite possibly the key document for comprehending our art since Matisse and Rimbaud), the young poet M, for something just over a week, devoted his evenings to a novel. Eventually published, some three years later, as *Events*, it attracted the attention of L, something of an Anglophile, who immediately translated the work into French under the title *Les effets*. Four years later, in somewhat different form, it was published in America as *Affairs*, whereupon it caught the interest of a young Argentine novelist whose command of English was firm (as exhibited in the multilingual puns of his own work), if a bit lacunal and over-refined; his translation, *La Feria*, appeared ten years after the book's initial publication. The following year it came out in Italy, and was twice reprinted, as *La lealtà*. Gradually it traveled to Germany, Yugoslavia, China, Russia (where it remained in print for fifteen years and was filmed by a cousin of Eisenstein), Czechoslovakia, Greece, Sweden, India and Japan. It finally reached Poland, where one of the many rising and remarkably talented young writers of the *List* group (who for the main part, following the example of

Mrozek, Herbert and others, wrote something neither
prose nor poetry, though close perhaps to the récit—a
kind of plotless, poetic allegory at several removes) devoted two years to its translation. Though multilingual—
fluent in French, Italian, Spanish, English, German and
Serbo-Croatian; a capable reader of Russian, Classical
Greek and Latin, Turkish—O felt his command of English
inadequate to the "intense subtlety" of the book and,
during the course of his translation (unaware of the
Czech translation's existence), had cause to refer to various editions of the work. The result of his efforts, *Oc-
zekiwałem niemożliwe przygody*, was upon publication
widely acclaimed, secured his reputation for once and all,
and transformed the aspirations of the entire *List* group.
That same year a Polish friend living in Paris, an established literary figure who had corresponded with O at
great length during his work at the novel, persuaded his
French publisher to issue a new edition of the book in a
translation of his own. By this time the novel was univer-
sally recognised as a classic—"one of the ten great novels
in world literature"—despite its length, which exceeded
that of *Estimations* by a single page. It seemed, however,
that the original edition of both the British and American
versions had been pulped, that there was a copy available
nowhere; and the London publisher A&B found it necessary to commission a translator, who worked from the
great variety of editions available, chiefly the French,
Polish and Russian, eventually condensing his 600-odd
pages of draft, notes and manuscript to a volume of just
over 200 closely printed pages. In a grand flourish of
promotion quite atypically British, this was brought out
some thirty or more years after its writing under the title
The Vacant Blood, subsequently reissued in America

(where it was a bestseller), and became the standard edition. It was generally believed at this time that the author was dead; whereas in reality, now over fifty, he lived in Manchester, in a crumbling colonial cottage to which were admitted but a few select friends, none of them writers, and even they solely by invitation. His poems continued to appear, infrequently, in only the most obscure and élite journals. By chance one day a copy of *The Vacant Blood* came into his possession. He sat up late on several successive evenings; it was the first book he had attempted to read in well over ten years. And though he understood little of it, he liked and admired—and yes, envied—this strange novel quite a lot indeed.

V

Kazoo

Walking down the street on my way to see The Leech,
I'm attacked by this guy who jumps out of the alley
shouting *Hai! Hai! Feefifofum!* (you know: bloodcur-
dling) over and over, cutting air with the sides of his
hands. He says *Hai!* again, then *Watch out, man! I'm
gonna lay you open!* He's still assaulting the air, battering
it too.

My, I think, *an alley cat.* Then I stand off and kind of
watch this little dance he's doing. Dispassionately in
front, you see, but I get to admiring it. I mean, he's
cutting some great steps, beating hell out of the air. I snap
my fingers for him, clap a little.

You watch out, man! he says. *You get cute, I'm gonna
hurt you bad, put you through that wall there.* Then he
goes back to his *Hai!* and *Feefifofum!* He's standing off

about three yards from me, jumping around, chopping his hands back and forth, looking mean, a real hardankle. He's about five foot and looks like he might have modeled for Dylan Thomas' bit about the "bunched monkey coming."

By this time there's quite a crowd piling up. They're all standing around clapping, snapping their fingers, digging the action. Some guy in like black heads in to sell *Watchtowers* and this Morton pops up and starts passing around stone tablets and pillows of salt. There's a spade out on the edge of the crowd, he's picking pockets, got three arms. Deep Fat Friar passes by, frowns, goes on down the street flogging himself with a vinyl flyswatter. And there's this cop on the fringe giving out with a mantra of dispersal. *Ibishuma, go go; Ibishuma, go go* (don't think he had it quite right, you know?).

One guy pulls out a set of plastic spoons and commences to make them go clackety-clack, clackety-clack between his thumb and great toe. Another guy has a kazoo. Someone else is trying to get them to do Melancholy Baby. *Take your clothes off and be adancin' bare*, this smartass yells out of the back of the crowd. He *is* kinda hairy, this guy.

Come on, Ralph, he shouts at me. *Come on, man, we're gonna tangle. Hai! Feefifofum!* But you can tell he likes it, the attention I mean, because he goes up on his toes and pirouettes.

I stand there looking at him, frowning a little, dispassionate again. I mean, I'm getting kind of tired of the bit by now. Some guy comes by about then with a monkey on his back, grinding at a nutchopper. Another one's hunkered-down on the corner to demonstrate his Vegamatic; his buddy's scraping bananas. And there's this like arthritic wobbling down the sidewalk with a Dixie cup, begging green-stamps.

Hai! Hai! Hing! (that last one way up in the nose).

He stops and drops his hands, looks down at the concrete, shuffles his feet. *Aw come on Ralph.* . . . Then he's *Hai!*-ing and *Feefifofum!*-ing again, going at it like mad, jumping around like a spastic toad.

And by this time I'm beginning to get *real* tired. I mean, I put up with his bag through here but now I'm gonna be late to see The Leech, so I—and let this be a lesson to all of you—I move in for the kill. I've been watching Captain Conqueroo on the morning tube, you see, and I'm like eager to try this thing out. So when this guy sees me coming and charges in like a rhinoceros or something, I just step ever so casually to one side and with a sudden blur of motion I get him with the Triple-Reverse Elbow Block, lay it right on him. He folds up like a letter that's getting put in an envelope that's too small for it and he falls down in like slow motion. His tongue's hanging out and a fly's walking up it toward his teeth.

Name's not Ralph, I tell him. Then I stand there humming along with the spoons and kazoo till he can breathe again. Which doesn't take him over twenty minutes or so —we'd only got through Black Snake Rag, Mountain Morning Moan, and part of America the Beautiful (raga form).

Anyhow, he starts coming back from violet toward the pinkish end of the spectrum, and he looks up at me and he says, *Aw gee, Algernon. Look, give me a chance. Sorry I bugged you.* Saying that reminds him of something and he stops long enough to spit out the fly. *Wasn't my idea,* he goes on. *Nothing personal against you, guy told me to do it . . . Bartholomew?*

I shake my head. I kick him a little. *Who.*

Guy just came up to me at the bus stop, told me you were on your way to the bank, don't know who he was. Said if I beat you up I could have the money and if I didn't he'd send his parakeet out to get me . . . Chauncey?

I kick him again. *Big guy? Southerner? Hair looked like a helmet? Scar where his nose should be, cigar stuck in it?*

Yeah . . . Look, you wouldn't be Rumplestiltskin by any chance?

Sorry. I tell him that as I'm kicking him.

Didn't think so.

I reach down to help him up, since he's obviously going to need help. *That'd be Savannah Rolla, a friend of mine,* I tell him. Savvy's a film-maker and I know he and a poet-type by the name of Round John Virgin are hassling with a love epic called *Bloodpies*—in which the symbols of the mudcake, the blood bath, the cow patty, and innocent youth find their existential union—so I look around for the cameras. But I can't spot them.

I'm on my way to the blood bank, I tell the guy. *He's got a funny sense of humor, Savannah does. Do anything for a friend, though.* And since his hand's in mine anyway since I'm helping him up, I shake it.

Ferdinand Turnip, I introduce myself. *Ferdinand. My wife is a Bella, name's Donna.*

Percival Potato, he says, and gives me this big grin like he's busting open. *Mad to greet you.* He's giving me the eye, so I take it and put it in my wallet right next to the finger someone gave me the day before.

We talk a while, have lunch together in the laundromat, then it's time for me to split. We notice the band's still going at it and Percy cops a garbage can and heads over to blow some congadrum with them. I walk a mile, catch a camel, and rush to the blood bank. I realize I've left all my beaver pelts at home again, so I take off one of my socks (the red one) and give it to the driver. He blows his nose on it, thanks me, and puts it in his lapel.

At the blood bank Dr. Acid, who's the head, tells me The Leech is dead from overeating. Dr. Acid has three friends: Grass, who's rooting around in the drawers; Roach, who looks like a leftover; and Big H, who rides a horse—Joint has the bends and is taking the day off. They're all eating popcorn balls and scraping bits of The Leech off the wall, putting the pieces in a picnic basket that has a place for bottles of wine too. They ask me to stay for a potluck dinner, but I say no. I cop some old commercials with them for a while, then I dive out of the window and swim to my studio. Someone's dumped Jello in the water, and it's pretty tough going. The crocs are up tight today, but the piranha seem placid enough.

At the studio, reverently, I apply the 65th coat to my *Soft Thing*—four more to go. I got the idea from Roy Biv, a friend of mine. Each layer of paint is a step up the spectrum, a solid color. I have carefully calculated the weight of my paint, canvas, medium. The last brush stroke of the 69th coat, and my painting will fall through the floor. It will be a masterpiece of aesthetic subtlety.

By the time I've drunk all the turpentine and finished burning the brushes, it's willy-nilly time to dine. But the lemmings are bad in the hall so I'm late catching my swan and I have to wait on top of the TV antenna for over an hour. Then by the time I get home, the vampires are out. They wave as I pass. Everyone knows you can't get blood from a Turnip—and anyway, they're all saps.

I go in and Donna comes up and kisses me and puts her

arm around me and tells me she doesn't love me anymore. I look out the window. Sure enough, the world's stopped going 'round.

So I go in the john and find my kazoo and I play for a long time.

The Creation
of Bennie Good

"Do you like my foot," putting it on the table. There,
between the chipped saucer and candle; you have noticed
how carefully I avoid the marmalade, the box of salty
butter. "Will you accept it as a token of my affection? For
you? It is, as they say, a good foot." Earlier, I have deftly
undone the laces with my toes, grasped the sock between
piano-key toes and foot and slowly drawn it off, like
peeling a willow wand. "The arch is long and graceful,
with the springy delicacy of a light man. The toes curl in
as though to embrace the foot; the nails are flecked with
color. And pink is the color of this foot." Pink, with the
bright red crescent at the top of the curve: pimple on one
side, in the curve, and dimpled on the other. "I am offering this, should you want it, my dear. It is all I have."

Her attention is arrested by my foot. This is true of

most. At parties my friends will group together talking,
and glancing occasionally with great expectation toward
the corner chair where I sit calm, unmoved, unmoving. As
the evening advances, their glances are more frequent
and begin to form a rhythm; then finally, beginning as a
low moan among the women, gradually swelling up
through the groups until it becomes a steady, hard, synco-
pated shout, and bursting at last out of the crowds, the
call comes: *Foot! Foot!* Then slowly I lift it to the level of
their eyes and one of them, a woman, the chosen, comes
forward out of the group wearing shyness like a belt and
starts softly to undo the pale pink shoe, dropping it to the
floor, where it lies on its side in the carpet pile. You have
seen the way a snake is skinned—first the skin is slit away
from the mouth, then rolled gently down along the body:
this is how my sock is removed—then thrown to them. A
few are unable to stand the pressure and must be sent
away. Others on the edge near me remove their own shoes
and socks and sit staring sadly at the pale uncovered feet.
I tell her all this.

"It's all I have, it's yours." But this one, this Sally, is
more moved than the rest. Already the tight black circles
around her eyes are smearing, becoming less distinct;
eyelids covered in green sequins are flashing like tiny
chandeliers. Her little hands are perched on the rim of the
cup and soon one will creep out across the ceramic dishes
to shyly, lightly touch my foot. She is overwhelmed at the
size of the occasion, the depth of my offer.

Perhaps I will make conversation; I've found this sometimes helps, especially in the initial slight embarrassment.
I will discuss various projects.

Such as . . .

Last year I had a large number of foam-rubber genitalia prepared for me by an advertising firm. These were bright pink and varied in size from two feet to six in length, and from a few inches to several yards in circumference. The order was placed on a Monday after a weekend of planning and sketching; on Thursday the genitalia were ready; and on Friday I set out for Niagara Falls with them packed away in my trunk. When I opened the trunk later, at the hotel, the genitalia expanded—virtually exploded—out into my room, filling it. Some had got tangled together, like fingers in doughnuts. That evening I fought my way through the foam to go out and walk among the people, talking to many and asking questions. And the next morning, when the sun was gleaming on the water, I walked with my trunk to the top of the Falls and floated my collection of vast foam genitals down toward all the people below: they bobbed and raged on the water.

Or. I will have a simulacra head made of intelligent clay—in my image precisely, though perhaps a touch more worldly, without the elusive pale delicacy of my own features. With great patience I will teach this head to say Yes, and I will keep it in a wooden box, a box of dogwood, on my left shoulder. Whenever I am asked a question requiring response, I will reach up across my chest and open the door to this box. The head will open its eyes, say Yes—and I will shut the door.

I will train crickets to function as metronomes and place one with every violinist in the world, thus restoring natural order to contemporary music.

By lies and deceit I have caused the Atlantic and Pacific Oceans to become jealous of one another; already they are creeping across America toward a confrontation. Frantically I have this morning cabled the Dead Sea, entreating it to intervene. Which it will.

And she listens. Even as lorries load cans in the alley and roll away, scraping long grooves in the bricks on each side, as the photographers shyly cover their lenses with their hands, as the waiters come and go, replacing dishes, bringing fresh flowers in vase after vase, the clack-clack of them in their rubber shoes. She listens.

And I tell her again, does she understand: "I am a ruined man. This is all I have left. And this, I offer to you." We sit for several minutes listening to corks pop off bottle after bottle around us, like children pulling fingers out of puffed cheeks. They have worked a long time for this; we are at last together. When I look at them, they raise their glasses toward us in celebration. Quickly, more bottles are brought in. A serving cart full of jangling green and clear, that hums and glides too slowly in front of the trotting waiter. More corks, soda, bubbles cascade into glasses, cubes of ice pop up like fishheads and the bubbles resemble their eyes. Me straight in the chair with a high head talking. Admiring how she maneuvers the delicate machinery of eggcup and spoon.

When I am finished she calls softly for the table to be cleared. With a wave of her hand, and light winks in the rings. The band stops and all is quiet as the waiters come and depart with full arms. I am finished. The lights go up, a few people stand for a better view.

She sits straight. So straight like a Cézanne cypress, and hardly anyone breathes now as, smiling, she moves back in her chair and adjusts the top of her body. We hear the gentle, crisp sound of her skirts. . . .

Finally I lift my head out of my wet hands. There is little energy left, in me.

And now there are cheers, calls of approval, relief. She is smiling. Staring straight into my eyes and nothing moves. The green folds of her skirt are pulled back, arranged around her waist and legs like a monster lettuce, and there on the veined-marble table, square in the center by my own, she has put her foot. Her tiny foot is offered, there.

And on it, the most exquisite black shoe.

Jane Crying

This is my wife in the blue window crying. And my son in the room behind her playing with his Christmas toys. As you can see, she is wearing only a delicate yellow bra and even at this distance you can tell how soft and smooth her brown skin will be. When you touch it. That first time.

※

As I recall, we met while skydiving. I came out of the plane after her, fell free until I was just above the silk mushroom of her parachute, then pulled the cord of my own kit. I believe we discussed Kant on the way down. That is to say, the categorical imperative.

※

But she is not crying. She is laughing. They are all laughing. Jane, Pam, Barbara, Pat, Chris. They are all together in bed. Happy and laughing. They are drawing straws tonight. Pam draws the short one. The others use their own straws to tease her erogenous zones, of which she has more than her fair share. This is to excite her sexually. So she will be ready. When I come. At the height of her passion.

*

My wife is sitting in an expensive Danish chair. It is her parents' chair. In her parents' home. She is sitting before the fireplace in which they burned the gift wrappings last night but there's no fire now. Only the light on the snow. The light of the moon, a clean cold light. She is trying to keep from thinking about thinking about crying. About me.

*

For years then I didn't see her. Till one day, skindiving off Bermuda, and a shark approached. As we had been well taught, we swam together directly towards the shark and thumped it on the nose, whereupon it fled. Naturally this shared experience created an instant bond between us. She invited me to her cabana for a drink and we talked over old times. Later we dined together and she introduced me to my son. The following day we were married.

*

This is my wife at a party with someone. She is wearing a dazzling low-cut Neiman Marcus gown and has somehow contrived to have breasts. Her hair is blonde and she is wearing a fall, piled and twined into an intricate coiffure atop her head. There are pink pearls resting against her skin, the soft brown skin at the base of her neck. She is smiling and slightly drunk on Brandy Alexanders. Perhaps this is not my wife at all.

❊

Kate. Joanna. Hilary. Pam. Carol. Crystine. Renée. Wynn.

56 Ridgemount Gardens. 141 East 13th. 6 rue de Tournon. 221 Camden High Street. Houston and Delancey. Cracow. Juarez. Harlem. Rio. Milford.

❊

She hasn't heard from me for several years and received this morning a copy of *Certains,* a collection of poems written in French published last year in Paris and dedicated to her. A Jane, à jamais. The first section is titled "Poésies pour la mort." She has been trying all day to read it. Now she is reading one of the books I gave her. *L'écume des jours.* She reaches the end, cries, reads it again. She is reading the last chapter with her eyes closed. Tears are coming out from under the lids.

❊

Marc. Gary. Ted. John. Terry. André. Marek. Bob.

5430 Wateka Drive. 331 Harvard Street. 18 Orchard

Street. 6918 Philadelphia Avenue. Dallas. Cambridge. Boston. Mexico City. Washington. Dallas.

❀

Now she is crying because she is in a white gown at a wedding. Because we are being married again. My son is the best man.

❀

She is crying again. Our son has left to find me. He believes I am in Paris and has flown there to bring me back. He is 12.

❀

This is my wife at her first one-man show in a Boston gallery. She has lost weight and is wearing a trousersuit. Her hair is black. She is wearing glasses. She is beautiful. She is crying because they are buying all of her paintings.

❀

Jane. Gail. Cambridge.
Jim. Julio. Argentina.

❀

She takes the news quite well. *Missing in action.* This is my wife in the blue window crying. It was the least I could do.

Bubbles

D——, where are you now?

I've searched for you down in the cove, by the little sandstone temple that the Greek built when his daughter married, where a wild cat lives, all butter and ginger; in the Soho pubs and Hampstead house parties; down by the docks where the air smells of banana, oil floats out on the water (Ophelia's gowns), and spiders crept across the top of my black shoes that stood like open graves on the whitewashed boards.

Once, I asked after you at the small café on the bridge by Paddington Station and a man in the corner, overhearing, paused with a forkful of soft dry cheese in front of his mouth (his forefinger nicotine-stained halfway down between the joints) and spoke across the room through already-parted lips: "Kilroy, you say? Ah yes, he was here. Remember him well; almost like my own son, he was. Yes, he was here"—then delivered the fork and chewed: a mouthful of crumbling custard. On the brown table beside him sat his teeth, poundnotes clenched between them, a pink moneyclip in the morning sun.

("Love, hate, indifference," you used to say in your flamboyant way, "they can work wonders, miracles. If you have belief." And—flamboyantly, extravagantly—I believed. In you. And now have only this, all this guilt, that bangs away inside me.)

Outside the café now, four men point in four directions and step backwards until they come together. A delivery boy in white pedals along the bridge and stops before me, returning undelivered another of the cables by which I have tried to reach you:

> Yesterday the cows came
> home stop Bailey expected
> later today stop Where
> are you stop

On the opposite wall of the bridge someone has spray-painted *Kilroy the saviour*. "Is it true, sir?" the delivery boy asks. "Can he really do all they say he can?" I go over and scrape the white letters off into an envelope, marking it *near Paddington Station, 4 Jan, 6 AM*. Does this mean he has left the city? A lorry comes by, killing the delivery boy, who has tried to follow me across the street.

And so I go walking down Westbourne Grove where teddy bears hang by their ears on the clotheslines, where marzipan elephants lounge in the palms of children and American Indians camp in the dustbins, their salty, tee-pee smoke spiraling up between the Queen Anne houses.

Leaning against one of the spear fences, a flophatted old man blows his nose into a tiny rag of flannel then holds it out away from his eyes, looking to see what he's brought up, like a fisher, from the deeps. "Hey, got a sixpence?"— and his huge nostrils hang there in front of my face like two black holes in the morning. As always, walking—its regularity, the rhythm of it—brings me to another kind of rhythm; I always end up singing or, in busier parts of the city, humming quietly to myself. So now as I walk (hopefully toward you) over the gobbets of paint and the heelspores of crushed orange chalk, past the walls and fences painted with six-foot flowers and diminutive Chinese dragons, past the bakeshops with their pastel façades, I'm singing softly to myself *Jesus wants me for a sunbeam*.

Who would have thought it. When we squatted together in piles of dust behind the books upstairs, sharing the last disposable yellow paper robe (luckily a 44, so it fitted us perfectly) and nibbling at the cake of vanilla seaweed we found in a drawer when we took the flat? That you should leave, and months later the realization of what had happened would come so suddenly upon me, and with such force, that I would sit for days without moving or speaking, until friends came at last and carried me away. That finally, obsessed with the depth of my guilt and loss, I should come searching for you, asking everywhere, sending these messages out ahead of me (cables, phonecalls, bits of paper thrown out the window to passers-by), out from my tiny room in Clapham Common, and following these signs across all of London: chalk on brick walls, letters sprayed from cans, empty chocolate wrappers which could be yours. . . .

On the street in front of a fish shop two children are

killing one another with wooden swords while all the silver-bubble fisheyes watch them calmly and dogs sit across the street quietly looking on. Farther down, where wind has rattled windows, a burglar alarm clangs. In this amazing new stillness a young man enters a nearby dentist's office ("Half a pint, sir? Three bob, please; just put this over your face") and emerges giggling. The window is filled with old dental tools, toppling in lines off the velvet-covered shelves and looking like instruments for exquisite torture: the relics of orbicular inquisitions.

In Notting Hill Gate (I wonder if you remember this) the buildings catch the wind and lay it like a ribbon down along the pavement; it swirls about my ankles, clinging, resilient, as I tramp through. Three one-man bands glare at one another from the corners of an intersection, waiting for the light. The flowerseller's black Alsatian is wearing a chain of daisies at its neck; it can catch pennies on its tongue. Remembering the old man's nostrils on Westbourne Grove, I make for the tube station—then bump bump bump (down the funny stairs from the tipitittitop). One wall is covered with telephone numbers; vast 69's scratched into the cement with belt-buckles or penknives; a poem in red shoe polish:

> During the raids
> the lost plane
> reported
> the war over
> the pilot missing

On the other, in a tiny elegant script, is penciled: *When Kilroy returns.* I stop and with people staring over my shoulder scrape the minute gray flakes off into an envelope.

The third level is deserted. I stand alone by the track, hearing the far-off rumble of trains and the dim, flat voices that float after me, tangling together, down the corridors behind. I turn to look down the rails and when I turn back, a cleaning machine is rushing toward me, its tiny mechanical arm erect out in front like a bull's horn. Quickly I step back against the wall, into the leering two-dimensional arms of a Chinese prostitute. "*Look out! Mind!*" the little machine shouts—penny-sized speaker rattling, distorting under the load—then pulls to a stop just past me and comes slowly backwards.

"Who," it asks (the arm quivering), "are you," (the arm stabbing out toward me). "I" (bending back on itself to point, dead center, at itself from above) "am The Machine. *Look out for The Machine!*" A pause. "I'll get you, you know; going to take your place, replace you, do away with your sort." (The arm stabs out again, almost to my knee.) "And about time, too. So *look out!* I'm giving you fair warning now!"

It starts away; then stops, purrs a moment and returns, the little treads lugging sadly backwards.

"What are you doing here!" it demands. "Let me see your passport! Would you like your shoes shined. They need it. I have some nice red polish."

I back away from the arm.

"Kilroy," I say quickly. "Have you seen him; has he been here?"

"Kilroy! You know Kilroy! Yes, he was here!" The little machine pauses, waving its arm thoughtfully. "*He* listened to me. We used to sit here for hours, talking over philosophical problems—mostly ethics, I remember. That was before he went away." The arm droops. "A good man. Sometimes, thinking about a man like that, it almost

makes me want to forgive you for everything. Almost."
The arm suddenly springs back to life, full of excitement.
"Do you know where he is!"

"I'm afraid not. I'm trying to find him."

The arm wilts again. "The only one who ever had
enough sense, enough compassion, to listen. *He* knew I
was right. . . ."

"When I do, I'll let you know, and tell him that you
asked after him." I turn and start back up the corridors,
but the little machine shoots around in front of me.

"Just a moment," it says. "I'm supposed to give you a
riddle, you know, before I can let you go." It sits for
several minutes, the tiny arm flopping and waving, in
deep thought. "But I can't think of one just now. Would
you like to hear me clap my hand. I suppose it's all right
for you to pass, since you know Kilroy. But I should have
something done about those shoes if I were you."

I walk up the tunnel. Behind me the little cleaner
shouts: "You don't have much time left, you know. *Watch
out for The Machines!*"—and goes zooming away down
the concrete beside the tracks. The last syllable had
blurred, rattling like a cough; apparently the speaker had
finally been too much strained, and the diaphragm had
cracked.

I climb back up past all the posters of girls in yellow
swimwear and the ticket machines into the crowds. It's
five now, and the streets are full of dogs. As I walk past a
row of phonebooths outside a Wimpy Bar, one of the
phones rings. I beat the others there and pick it up:

"Yes?"

"We've found him." Outside, it's raining; this booth
contains me perfectly, with the water breaking on the
gray glass, destroying the world outside.

"Where?"

"There's been an accident. Mercy Hospital. He's asking for you. Hurry." The rain is washing cigarette butts up under the door and into the booth. On a minicab sign someone has written on the cab's window: *He slept here.* Not bothering this time to collect the sign, I ring for a cab.

At the hospital I'm greeted by a nurse in layers of diaphanous white that slide over one another, with pink somewhere underneath. She's painted black rims around her eyes, and has a pink-white mouth.

"This way, hurry. He's been asking for you. It may be all that's keeping him alive, making him hold on."

We go down white tile halls where everyone else walks near the walls; the center is new and clean. Then into a room full of soft murmurs and liquid sounds. Five surgeons squat in one corner talking together quietly. A nurse kneels by the bedside crying. Outside the window four young girls stand still and straight, and sing.

He lies on the bed under a clear plastic tent, with the sheets pulled up to his chin. All around him the air is filled with tubes and small, pumping engines. Fluids run bubbling through the tubes; go slowly down, and more quickly up, along them. It's as though his blood system, lymph system—all the delicate soft machinery of his body —has been brought out into the world, redirected through glass and plastic. He is larger than the rest of us. (I remember the long months I lay still and dazed, recovering from the loss of your leaving. Perhaps it was here that I lay. My guilt sustains me.)

When the nurse folds back a flap in the tent he opens his eyes, and I hear the soughing of the pumps more distinctly.

"You . . . came." When he speaks, the fluids run faster in the tubes, gurgling in time with his voice. Bubbles forming, bursting, passing slowly, like fisheyes, along the tubes.

"I . . . told them . . . you would." His eyes are gray, pupil and iris barely distinguishable from the rest. It occurs to me now that he can see nothing; I could be anyone; it wouldn't matter. (And how you smiled and brought coffee and talked to me quietly. Your face was always so different, so changed, in the dark.)

"I . . . knew you . . . would." There is a gentle hissing as the nurse opens the oxygen valve a degree wider. (The way I stood at the window, watching, not yet understanding. Afterwards, the room seemed . . . larger. I was aware of the space between things.)

"Bless . . . you."

Fluids jumped in the tube (*bubble bubble bubble:* the rhythm of a laugh) and now are still, as the pumps shut off. There is only the hiss of oxygen coming into the tent, out into the room. One huge bubble hangs motionless at the bend of a tube, watching.

"Is he dead?"

The nurse goes over to speak with the doctors. They listen carefully, tilting their heads toward her, and nod. The nurse returns:

"Yes."

So I go into the hall and stand there looking out at the polished green grass and flowers in the hospital lawn. A vine which has climbed the building is now blossoming, scattering leaves down into the yard. It looks like the veins in a hand. Flowers climb along it toward the roofs.

"I'm sorry. . . ." She comes up behind me.

"You needn't be. It wasn't him."

"Then who? Your guilt——"

"I don't know." I turn to face her. The pink-white lipstick is smudged at one corner of her mouth. Should I tell her? How much she resembles his wife; that this may have made it easier for him, near the end? "I don't know who he was. I've never seen him before." I start down the hall and she comes after me.

"Please. Just a moment. This." She holds out a large manila envelope: bulky, jangling. "His personal effects, what he had in his pockets. I wonder . . . could you take them? Please." I take the envelope from her and leave. Hardly anyone in the halls now. The sun is slanting in through the window, moving out across the tiles. When I turn my head to look back at the vine, it almost blinds me. But the flowers are spilling up over the edge of the roof.

Later, on the street, I open the envelope and spread the things out on top of a low wall. It contains: thirty-nine ha'pennies, two sixpences marked EM in red ink, a child's gyroscope top, and a number of small white envelopes containing bits of paint and graphite, each with a place and date scrawled on the outside.

Farther along the wall in black chalk: *We shall be reborn.* Conceivably. But I've used all my envelopes. The only unsealed one I have is the one with the dead man's things—so I scrape the chalk off into that and mark it *Mercy.* (Tomorrow I will have to return to the phone-booth.) And go walking softly down the street toward home. With a song in my mouth.

Like eyelids, all the windows are open, rolled up on their cords.

And night blooms over the heads of the buildings.

A FEW LAST WORDS

What is the silence
   a. As though it had a right to more
                              —W. S. Merwin

   Again:
He was eating stained glass and vomiting rainbows. He
looked up and there was the clock moving toward him,
grinning, arms raised in a shout of triumph over its head.
The clock advanced; he smelled decay; he was strangled
to death by the hands of time. . . . He was in a red room.
The hands of the clock knocked knocked knocked without entering. . . . And changed again. The hours had
faces, worse than the hands. He choked it was all so quiet
only the ticking the faces were coming closer closer he
gagged screamed once and—

   Sat on the edge of the bed. The hall clock was ticking
loudly, a sound like dried peas dropping into a pail. This
was the third night.
   The pumpkin-color moon dangled deep in the third

quadrant of the cross-paned window. Periodically clouds would touch the surface and partly fill with color, keeping it whole. Dust and streaks on the window, a tiny bubble of air, blurred its landscape; yellow drapes beside it took on a new hue.

He had watched it for hours (must have been hours). Its only motion was a kind of visual dopplering. It sped out into serene depths, skipped back in a rush to paste itself against the backside of the glass, looking like a spot of wax. Apogee to perigee to apogee, and no pause between. Rapid vacillation, losing his eyes in intermediate distances, making him blink and squint, glimmering in the pale overcast. And other than that it hadn't moved. Abscissa +, ordinate +. Stasis.

This was the third night.

His wife stirred faintly and reached to touch his pillow, eyelids fluttering. Hoover quickly put out his hand and laid it across her fingers. Visibly, she settled back into blankets. In the hall, the clock ticked like a leaking faucet. The moon was in its pelagic phase, going out.

The third night of the dreams. The third night that lying in bed he was overcome by: Presence. In the dark it would grow around him, crowding his eyes open, bunching his breath, constricting—at last driving him from the bed, the room. He would pace the rugs and floors, turn back and away again on the stairs, wondering. He would drink liquor, then coffee, unsure which effect he wanted, uneasy at conclusions—certain only of this sense of cramping, of imposition. In the dark he was ambushed, inhabited, attacked again from within.

His wife turned in bed, whispering against sheets, taking her fingers away.

Hoover lifted his head to the dresser, chinoiserie chair,

sculpt lamé valet, to glazed chintz that hid the second, curiously small window. A simple room, sparse, clean, a room with no waste of motion. And a familiar room, intimate and informal as the back of his hand, yet his eyes moving through it now encountered a strangeness, a distortion. He cast his vision about the room, tracing the strangeness back to its source at the window: to pale plastic light that slipped in there and took his furniture away into distances. It occurred to him that he was annoyed by this intrusion, this elusive division of himself from his things. He watched the moon and it stared back, unblinking.

Hoover fixed his chin between his fists, propped elbows on knees, and became a sculpture. His face turned again to see the window, head rolling in his hands, ball-in-socket.

A cave, he thought: that was the effect. Gloom, and moonlight sinking through cracks: pitch and glimmer. A skiagraphy of the near and foreign. Quarantine and communion, solitude and confederation. A cave, shaped in this strange light.

And bruising the light's influence, he walked to the chair and stared down at the suit he'd draped over one arm—looked at the hall clock—ten minutes ago. It was happening faster now. . . .

The suit was pale, stale-olive green and it shined in a stronger light. The coat barely concealed the jutting, saddle-like bones of his hips; his wrists dangled helplessly away from the sleeve ends like bones out of a drumstick— and Cass hated it. Regardless of fit, though, it *felt* right: he was comfortable in it, was himself.

He took the coat from the chair, held it a minute, and put it back. Somehow, tonight, it seemed inappropriate, like the man-shaped valet that no one used. As with the room, the furniture, it had been taken away from him.

He turned and shuffled across the rug to search through the crow-black corner closet behind the creaking, always-open door, discovering a western shirt with a yoke of roses across its breast and trying it on, then jeans, belting them tightly, and boots. The clothes were loose, looser than he remembered, but they felt good, felt right.

Stepping full into light at the door, he shattered strangeness, and looking back saw that the moon was now cockeyed in the corner of the pane.

Ticking of a clock, sound of feet down stairs.

He assassinated death with the cold steel rush of his breathing. . . .

The night was pellucid, a crystal of blackness; hermetic with darkness. He moved within a hollow black crystal and up there was another, an orange separate crystal, bubble in a bubble. . . . And quiet, so quiet so still, only the ticking of his feet, the whisper of breath. He pocketed his hands and wished for the coat he'd left behind.

Hoover turned onto the walk, heels clacking (another death: to silence).

A sepulchral feeling, he thought, to the thin wash of light overlaying this abyss of street. A counterpoint, castrati and bass. Peel away the light and you: Plunge. Downward. Forever.

Another thought . . . you can tell a lot by the way a person listens to silence.

(Sunday. It was evening all day. Over late coffee and oranges, the old words begin again. The speech too much used, and no doors from this logic of love. We go together like rain and melancholy, blue and morning. . . .)

At the corner, turn; and on down this new abyss. Breath pedaling, stabbing into the air like a silent cough, feet killing quiet—

I am intruding.

Darkness is avenging itself on my back.

(And I, guilty realist, dabbler at verses, saying: There is no sign for isolation but a broken spring, no image for time but a ticking heart, nothing for death but stillness. . . .)

Light glinted off bare windows. Most of the houses were marooned now in a moat of grass and ascending weed. Driveways and porches and garages all open and empty, dumbly grinning.

(Evening all day. World out the window like a painting slowly turning under glass in a dusty frame. Rain in the sky, but shy about falling. The words: they peak at ten, pace by noon, run out to the end of their taut line. . . .)

The shells have names, had them. Martin, Heslep, Rose. Walking past them now, he remembered times they were lit up like pumpkins, orange-yellow light pouring richly out the windows; cars, cycle-strewn yards, newspapers on steps. The casual intimacy of a person inside looking out, waving.

(And I remember your hair among leaves, your body in breaking dew, moonlight that slipped through trees and windows to put its palm against your face, your waist; bright and shadow fighting there. . . .)

Darkness. It moves aside to let you pass. Closes, impassable, behind you.

(Four times: you came to bed, got up, came back to bed. You turned three times, you threw the pillows off the bed. Michael, never born, who had two months to live, was stirring in you and stirring you awake.

Your hair was on the bed like golden threads. The moon had pushed your face up into the window and hidden your hands in shadow. You were yellow, yellow on the linen bed; and opened your eyes.

—If I weren't afraid, I could leave and never look back.

You say that, sitting in a hollow of bed, knees tucked to your flanneled breasts, arms around yourself.

—Would you follow, would you call me back?

I watch your steps track down the walk to the black, inviting street. And later, when I open the door, you're there, grinning, coming back; coming back to make coffee and wait for morning. And another night, another day, saved from whatever it is that threatens at these times. . . .)

Hoover looked at the streetlight shelled in rainbow and it was ahead, above, behind, remembered. Darkness shouldered itself back in around him. Snow hung in the air, waiting to fall. The dead houses regarded him as he passed, still, unspeaking.

(October, time of winds and high doubt. It comes around us like the shutting of a light: the same thing is happening to others. And the people are going away, the time has come for going away. . . . It all boils up in a man, and overflows. His birthright of freedom, it's the freedom to be left alone, that's what he wants most, just to be left alone, just to draw circles around himself and shut the world out. Every man's an island, why deny it, why tread water. So people let go. . . .)

Hoover picked the moving shape out of the alley and was down in a crouch, whistling, almost before the dog saw him. It raised its nose from the ground and walked bashfully toward him, sideways, tail banging at a drum, whining.

"Folks leave you, fella?" A brown shepherd with a heavy silver-studded collar; he didn't bother to look at the jangling nametags. "Take you home with me then, okay?" The shepherd whimpered its agreement. Hoover rummaging in his pockets.

"Sorry, fella, nothing to give you." Showing empty hands, which the dog filled with licks and nuzzles, snuffling.

"Bribery, eh. Sorry, still no food." He stroked his hand into the dog's pelt, found warmth underneath. It sat looking up at him, waiting, expecting, its tail swishing across pavement.

When he erected himself to full height, the dog jumped away and crouched low, ready to run. Hoover walked toward it and put out a hand to its broad, ridged head.

"It's okay, fellow. Tell you what. Come along with me to see a friend, then I'll take you right home and see about getting you something to eat. Think you can wait?"

They punctured the night together, down the walk, heels clacking, claws ticking. Hoover kept his hand on the dog's head as they walked. The nametags threw bells out into the silence.

"Or maybe he'll have something for you there, come to think of it."

Click, clack, click. Staccato tattooed on the ponderous night. The sky is still ambiguous.

(Remembering a night we sat talking, drinking half-cups of coffee as we watched stars sprinkle and throb and fade, then saw dawn all blood and whispered thunder. I remember how your eyes were, pink like shrimp, pink like the sky when it caught the first slanting rays and held them to its chest. And as morning opened around us we were talking of Thoreau and men who sailed the soul, of ways and reasons to change, the old orders, and of why things break up. Outside our window it was growing between them, people were letting go, were wanting their Waldens, their Innisfrees, their Arcadias, they were falling away from the town like leaves, like scaling paint, by twos, by ones. Even in our house, our hearts, it moves between us. Between us. We feel it turning, feel it touching. But we care, we love, we can't let go. . . .)

Hoover drew up short, listening. The shepherd beside him cocked its ears, trembled happily.

It happens like this . . .

A drone, far off. Closer. Becomes an engine. Then a swelling of light blocks away. Then a rush and churning and soon two lashing white eyes. Loudest, chased by a dog. A roar and past, racing. A thrown thing. Neil's car . . . and silence again.

And minutes later, the shepherd's body went limp and its head fell back onto his lap. Hoover took it in his arms and walked out of the road, its head rolling softly along the outside of his elbow. In the streetlight his face glistened where the dog had licked it.

Crossing the walk, kicking open a gate that wind had shut, Hoover surrendered his burden into the lawn. Ten steps away he looked back and saw that the dog's body was hidden in deep grass, secret as any Easter egg.

Three hundred and some-odd steps. Two turns. Five places where cement has split its seams, heaved up, and grass is growing in the cracks. Pacing this map . . .

(The sea grew tired one day of swinging in harness, ticking in its box of beach. One spark in the flannel sea, possessed of fury, gathering slime like a seeded pearl, thinks of legs and comes onto a rock, lies there in the sun drying. It seeps, it slushes, it creeps, it crawls; it bakes to hardness and walks. . . . All to the end: that I am walking on two feet down this corridor of black steel and my hand is turning like a key at this found door. . . .)

The door collapse-returned. He looked around. A single light cut into the café through a porthole of glass in the kitchen door; powdery twilight caught in the mirror. In the dim alley before him, neon signs circled and fell, rose and blinked across their boxes like tiny traffic signals. Profound, ponderous grayness, like the very stuff of thought. . . .

Decision failed him; he had turned to go when he heard the door and saw light swell.

"Dr. Hoover. . . ."

He turned back.

"Didn't know for sure you were still around." Nervously. "About the last ones, I guess."

Hoover nodded. "Any food, Doug?"

"Just coffee, sorry. Coffee's on, though. Made a pot for myself, plenty left." He stepped behind the counter and knocked the corner off a cube of stacked cups, burn scars on his hands rippling in mirror-bemused light.

"Sugar, cream?" Sliding the cup onto crisp pink formica.

Hoover waved them both off. "Black's the best way."

"Yeah. . . . No one been in here for a week or more. I ain't bothered to keep the stuff out like I ought to."

Hoover sat down by the cup, noticing that Doug had moved back away from the counter. "Like you say, I guess. Last ones."

Doug scratched at his stomach where it depended out over the apron. Large hands going into pockets, rumpling the starched white.

"Reckon I *could* get you a sandwich. Or some toast—then it don't matter if the bread's a little stale."

"Coffee's fine. Don't bother."

"You sure? Wouldn't be any trouble."

Hoover smiled and shook his head. "Forget it, just coffee. But thanks anyway."

Doug looked down at the cup. "Don't mind, I'll have one with you." His penciled monobrow flexed at the middle, pointed down. It was like the one-stroke bird that children are taught to draw; the upper part of a stylized heart. "Get my cup." Over his shoulder: "Be right back."

Light rose as the kitchen door opened; died back down, leaving Hoover alone. He turned his eyes to buff-flecked white tiles; let them carry his attention across the floor, swiveling his chair to keep up. Light picked out tiny blades of gleam on the gold bands that edged formica-and-naugahyde. A few pygmy neons hopscotched high on the walls. The booths were empty as shells, humming with shadow; above them (showing against homogenized paint, rich yellow, creamy tan; sprinkled among windows) were small dark shapes he knew as free-painted anchors.

(All this shut in a small café, sculpt in shades of gray. Change one letter, you have cave again. . . .)

Doug came back (light reached, retreated), poured steaming coffee. He squeezed around the end of the counter and sat two seats away.

"Neil left today."

"Yeah, I saw him up the street on the way here."

"So that's whose car it was. Wasn't sure, heard it going by. Going like a bat out of hell from the sound." He drank, made a face. "Too hot. Wonder what kept him? Said he was going to take off this morning." He blew across the mouth of his cup, as though he might be trying to whistle, instead breathing vapor. He tried another taste. "Will came through, you know. . . ."

Hoover's own cup was sweating, oils were sliding over the surface. It was a tan cup; the lip was chipped. They weren't looking at each other.

"That big cabin up on the cape. His grandfather built it for a place to get away and do his writing, way the hell away from everything. Now it's his."

"I know. My sister called me up last week to say good-bye, told me about it, they thought it was coming through. Wonder when *she's* leaving?"

Doug looked up sharply, then dropped his head. "Thought you knew. She left about three, four days ago." Doug belched, lightly.

"Oh. I guess she went up early to get things ready, he'll meet her there. You know women."

"Yeah. Yeah, that's probably it." He went for more coffee, poured for them both. "Coffee's the last thing I need."

"You too."

"Yeah—lot worse for some, though. Been over a week for me, lost about twenty pounds. Catnap some. . . . Thing you wonder about is, where'd they find a lawyer? For the papers and all. Didn't, maybe, guess it don't make much difference anymore, stuff like that. Anyhow, they're gone."

(And the wall's a wedge. Shove it between two people and they come apart, like all the rest. . . .)

Hoover shrugged his shoulders, putting an elbow on the counter and steepling fingers against his forehead.

"Almost brought a friend, Doug. . . ."

The big man straightened in his chair. His mouth made "Friend?" sit on his lips unspoken.

"But he was indisposed, disposed, at the last minute."

Doug was staring at him strangely.

"A dog. Neil hit it. I was going to see if I could talk you out of some food for it."

"Oh! Yeah, there's some stuff, meat and all I'm just gonna have to throw out anyway. What isn't spoiled already's getting that way fast. Didn't know there were dogs still around, though? Whose is it?"

"There aren't now. I hadn't seen it before. *Was* it: it's dead." Extinct.

"Oh. Yeah, Neil *was* going pretty fast. Dog probably wandered in from someplace else anyway, looking for food after they left him." Gazing into the bottom of his cup, Doug swirled what coffee was left against the grounds, making new patterns, like tiny cinders after a rain. "Always been a cat man myself. Couldn't keep one, though, haven't since I was a kid. Sarah's asthma, you know."

"You do have to be careful. Used to have hay fever myself, fall come around I couldn't breathe. Took an allergy test and they cleared it up."

"Yeah, we tried that. Tried about everything. You oughta see our income tax for the last few years, reads like a medical directory. Sarah got so many holes poked in her, the asthma should have leaked right out. Wasn't any of it seemed to help, though."

"How's Sarah doing? Haven't seen her for quite a while. She's usually running around in here helping you, shooing you back to the kitchen, making you change your apron, talking to customers. Brightens the place up a lot."

Doug tilted the cup to drain an extra ounce of cold coffee off the grounds.

"Not much business lately," he said. "Boy I had working for me just kind of up and left three-four months ago and I never got around to looking for help, no need of it, specially now."

"She's well, though? Doing okay."

Doug put his cup down, rattling it against the saucer.

"Yeah, she's okay. She—" He stood and made his way around the counter. "She went away a while. To get some rest." He dipped under the counter and came up with a huge stainless steel bowl. "Think I'll make another pot. This one's getting stale. Better anyhow if you use the stuff regularly, easier on it, works better—like getting a car out on the road to clean her out."

He started working at the urn, opening valves, sloshing dark coffee down into the bowl. Hoover watched Doug's reflection in the shady mirror and a dimmer image of himself lying out across the smooth formica.

So Doug's wife had gone away too; Sarah had gone to get some rest. . . . Hoover remembered a song he'd heard at one of the faculty parties: Went to see my Sally Gray, Went to see my Sally Gray, Went to see my Sally Gray, Said my Sally's gone away—only this time Sally Gray had taken everybody else with her. . . .

Doug was chuckling at the urn.

"You know I gotta make twenty cups just to get two for us, I mean that's the least this monster here'll handle. Ask him for forty-fifty cups, he'll give it to you in a minute.

But you ask him for two, just two little cups of coffee, and he'll blow his stack, or a gasket or something." He went back to clanging at the urn. "Reckon you can handle ten of 'em?" He started fixing the filter, folding it in half twice, tearing off a tiny piece at one corner. "Hell, there ain't enough people left in town to drink twenty cups of coffee if I was giving it away and they was dying of thirst. Or anywhere around here."

He bowed the filter into a cone between his hands, climbed a chair to install it, then came down and drew a glass of water, putting it in front of Hoover.

"That's for while you wait."

"I need to be going anyway, Doug. Have to get some sleep sooner or later."

Doug reached and retrieved Hoover's cup, staring at the sludge settling against the bottom. "One last cup."

"All right. One more."

One for the road. . . .

Doug bent and rinsed the cup, then got another from the stack and put it on the counter. He stood looking at the clean empty cup, wiping his hands against the apron. He lit a cigarette, nodding to himself, and the glowing red tip echoed one of the skipping neon signs on the wall behind him. He put the package on the counter and smiled, softly.

"You know, you could've sat right here and watched the whole thing happening. I mean, at first there'd be the usual group, but they were . . . nervous. You know: jumpy. They'd sort of scatter themselves out and every now and then the talk would die down and there'd be this quiet, like everybody was listening for something, waiting for something. Then a lot of them stopped coming, and the rest would sit all around the room, talking across to each other, then just sitting there quiet for a long time by themselves. Wasn't long before the regulars didn't come anymore—and you knew what was going on, you knew they were draining out of town like someone had pulled the plug.

"That was when the others started showing up. They'd come in with funny looks on their faces, all anxious to talk. And when you tried to talk to 'em, they'd be looking behind you and around the room and every once in a while they'd get up and go look out the window. And then they'd leave and you'd never see them again."

Hoover sat with his legs cocked back, toes on the floor, regarding the glass of water (the bubbles had nearly vanished). He nodded: he knew, he understood.

"For a while I got some of the ones that were coming through. I'd be in the back and I'd hear the door and come out, and there'd be this guy standing there, shuffling his feet, looking at the floor. He'd pay and take his coffee over in the corner, then the next time I looked around, he'd be gone—lot of them would just take it with them, to go. Then even that stopped."

(The people: they drip, trickle, run, pour, flood from the cities. They don't look back. And the ones who stay, try to fight it—they feel it growing in them worse than before. Turning in them, touching them, and they care they love they can't let go. But the harder they fight, the worse it is, like going down in quicksand, and the wall's a wedge: shove it between two people and they come apart, like all the rest, like all the rest of the world. . . .)

Doug found something on the counter to watch.

"One time during the War, the ship I was on went down on the other side and a sub picked us up. I still remember how it felt, being in that sub, all the people

packed in like sardines, stuffed into spaces between controls and motors. You'd think it would be full of noise,
movement. But there was something about being under
all that water, being closed in, something about the light
—anyway, something that made you feel alone, made you
want to whisper. I'd just sit in it and listen. Feel. And
pretty soon I'd start wanting them all to really go away, to
leave me alone. . . ."

Doug stood looking for a moment out one of the small
round windows past Hoover's shoulder.

"Yeah. Yeah, that's the way it is all right." Then his eyes
switched back to Hoover's cup. "I better go get that
coffee, just take it a minute to perk."

He picked up his cup and walked down the counter
toward the kitchen, running his hand along the formica.
The door swung back in, wobbled, stopped (light had
reached, retreated).

Hoover felt suddenly hollow; empty; squeezed. He
looked around. The room was a cave again.

Out in the kitchen, Doug moved among his stainless
steel and aluminum. Hoover heard him banging pots on
pans, opening doors, sliding things on shelves out of his
way. Then the texture of sound changed, sank to quiet,
became a silence that stretched and stretched. And seconds later, broke: the back door creaked open and shut
with a hiss of air along its spring, clicking shut.

(So now the quicksand's got Doug too, for all his fighting. Now he's gone with the rest, gone with Sally
Gray. . . .)

Outside in the alley angling along and behind the café,
Doug's Harley Davidson pumped and caught, coughed a
couple of times and whined away, one cylinder banging.

Hoover sat looking at the abandoned cup as silence came in to fill his ears. Then he heard the buzzing of electric wires.

The last grasping and their fingers had slipped.

The wedge was driven in, and they'd come apart. . . .

He stood, digging for a dime and finding he'd forgotten to fill his pockets, then walked to the register and punched a key. "No Sale" came up under the glass. There were two nickels and some pennies.

He fed the coins in (ping! ping!), dialed, and waited. The phone rang twice and something came on, breathing into the wires.

"Cass?"

Breathing.

Again: "Cass?" Louder.

Breathing.

"Cass, is that you?"

Silence.

"Who is this? Please. Cass?"

A small, quiet voice. "I'm afraid you have the wrong number."

A click and buzzing. . . .

After a while, he reached up and flipped out the change tray. As the lid slid away, a tarnished gray eye showed there: someone had left a dime behind.

Nine rings. Cass' voice in the lifted phone. Sleepy; low and smooth; pâté, ready for spreading.

"Cass?"

"Is that you, Bob? Where are you?"

"Doug's place. Be right home." The space of breath. "Honey . . ."

"Yes?"

"Get your bags packed, we're leaving tonight."

"Leaving?" She was coming awake. "Where——"

"I don't know. South maybe, climate's better. But maybe that's what everyone will think—anyway, we'll decide. Just get your things ready, just what you absolutely have to have. We can always pick up things we need in towns. There's a big box in the bottom of the utility closet, some of my stuff, some tools and so on I got together a while back. Put that with the rest—there's some room left in it you can use. I'll be right home. Everything else we'll need is already in the car."

"Bob. . . ."

"Just do it Cass. Please. I'll be right back, to help."

"Bob, are you sure——"

"Yes."

She paused. "I'll be ready."

He hung up and walked into the kitchen, came out again with a ten-pound sack of coffee under one arm. He started over the tiles toward the door, then turned back and picked up the cigarettes lying on the counter. He stood by the door, looking back down the dim alley: stood at the mouth of the cave, looking into distances (he'd seen a stereopticon once; it was much the same effect).

The tiny neons skipped and blinked dumbly in their boxes; the kitchen light glared against the window, fell softly along the mirror. Shadows came in to fill the café; sat at tables, slumped in booths, stood awry on the floor; watching, waiting. At the end of the counter, the blank tan cup silently surrendered.

He turned and switched the knob. Went through the door. Shut it behind him. The click of the lock ran away into the still air and died; he was locked into silence. . . .

Cautiously he assaulted the street's independence, heels ticking parameters for the darkness, the motive, the town. The sky hung low above his head.

(I walk alone. Alone. Men don't run in packs, but they run. . . . Death at the wheel expects his spin. Dark seeps in around the edges, winds rise in the caves of our Aeolian skulls, five fingers reach to take winter into our hearts, the winter of all our hearts)

And they came now in the darkness, they loomed and squatted about him, all the furnished tombs: this dim garden of rock and wood.

(Bars of silence. Score: four bars of silence, end on the seventh. See how they show on my white shirt among the roses. Bars and barristers of silence)

The quick blue spurt of a struck match. A cigarette flames, then glows, moving down the street into darkness.

(There is no sign for isolation but a broken spring, no image for time but a ticking heart, nothing for death but stillness . . . and the wall, the wedge, is splitting deeper but we'll hold, for a while we'll hold on, you and I)

He stood still in the stillness that flowed around him and listened to the hum of insects calling through the black flannel. As if in answer, clouds came lower.

(At the mouth of caves, turning. We can't see out far, in deep, but the time has come for going away the time has come for becoming. . . . At the mouth of caves, turning, and time now to enter the calm, the old orders. At the mouth of caves. Turning)

He walked on and his heels talked and the night came in to hush him.

He shouted out into the dark, screamed once out into silence—and it entered his heart.

He passed a pearl-gray streetlight, passed a graveyard lawn.

("Sudden and swift and light as that the ties gave, and we learned of finalities besides the grave." Is this how it feels, the instant of desertion—a vague epiphany of epochal stillness, primal quiet?)

Around him, scarcely sounding his echo, stood the shells of houses, like trees awaiting the return of dryads who had lost their way.

(The instant of desertion, the instance of silence)

The cigarette arced into the street and fell there, glowing blankly.

He bent his head and began to hurry.

And with a flourish, the snows began.